FINDERS
KEEPERS

ALSO BY
SHELLEY TOUGAS

The Graham Cracker Plot

FINDERS KEEPERS

Shelley Tougas

Roaring Brook Press
New York

Copyright © 2015 by Shelley Tougas
Published by Roaring Brook Press
Roaring Brook Press is a division of Holtzbrinck
Publishing Holdings Limited Partnership
175 Fifth Avenue, New York, New York 10010

mackids.com

Library of Congress Cataloging-in-Publication Data

Tougas, Shelley.
    Finders keepers / Shelley Tougas. — First edition.
        pages cm
    Summary: In Wisconsin, ten-year-old Christa and eleven-year-old Alex team
up to search for the lost treasure of Al Capone near where Alex has just moved
into his grandfather's house and Christa is spending what may be her family's
last summer in their cabin.
    ISBN 978-1-59643-990-0 (hardback) — ISBN 978-1-59643-991-7 (e-book)
    [1. Buried treasure—Fiction.   2. Adventure and adventures—
Fiction.   3. Friendship—Fiction.   4. Family life—Wisconsin—
Fiction.   5. Wisconsin—Fiction.]   I. Title.
    PZ7.T647155Fin 2015
    [Fic]—dc23
                                                        2015005138

Roaring Brook Press books may be purchased for business or promotional
use. For information on bulk purchases please contact Macmillan Corporate
and Premium Sales Department at (800) 221-7945 x5442 or by email
at specialmarkets@macmillan.com.

First edition 2015
Book design by Andrew Arnold
Printed in the United States of America by
R.R. Donnelley & Sons Company, Harrisonburg, Virginia

1 3 5 7 9 10 8 6 4 2

For Michael,
giver of laptops and love

SUMMER VACATION
AND THE THIEF

I glared at Olivia Stanger's picture on the for-sale sign. Her silver hair sparkled, and her big smile showed teeth as white as wedding cake frosting. Icky-sticky sweet.

So I karate kicked that sign, the sign that announced she was *selling my cabin*.

The sign swung away, but my foot kept going. I landed in the splits, then pressed my whole body against the grass. The sign swung back but missed my head. I was fast. Cougar fast.

Olivia Stanger had forced a stake into the ground

for her sign. A thin pole stuck out near the top of the stake, forming a backward number seven. The sign with her picture hung from the top of the seven. The icky-sticky-sweet smile was as wide as my head.

Next to me was a big stick, so I held it against the ground and pulled myself out of the splits. We were face-to-face again, me and Olivia Stanger's sign.

So I whacked her face with the stick.

Then I spit on the sign, right by the words that said, "Olivia Stanger, Your Wisconsin Lakeshore Realtor."

"What'd that sign ever do to you?"

The voice was a boy covered in mud. Mud on his hands, on his knees, on his green t-shirt. He stood in the grass a few feet from the gravel driveway.

I looked at the muddy boy, then the sign.

I wished Olivia herself would answer. Because if the for-sale sign were an evil talking sign, she'd say, "Miss Christa Boyd-Adams. I will make sure you'll be home every summer, stuck in arts-and-crafts camps. You'll make paper-bag dresses and sock puppets. WAH HA HA HA!"

From under the mud came the boy's voice again. "You got a problem with that sign?"

"Yeah, I got a problem with this sign. A big problem."

"That lady's face is on signs everywhere around here. I guess some people must like her."

"I guess they do. They must like a thief in a business suit selling their best stuff. The stuff they've had since they were born."

He eyed the cabin up and down. "It's not as nice as the places for sale in Arizona. That's where I'm from. But it's a decent cabin. Does it have an actual bathroom? With a toilet that actually flushes?"

"Of course it has a flushing toilet! It's not a hunting shack. It has electricity and a fireplace and two bedrooms. It even has closets."

He nodded. "Then you'll sell it for a wad of money."

Money. That's what my parents wanted. Money from the sale to pay bills. I'd rather sell our house, which was ten hours from the cabin, in a boring neighborhood with hardly any trees.

3

"Nobody should buy this place," I said. "If you're honest, you'll tell lookers the truth. Are you honest?"

"Guess so."

My brain had to work fast. Race-car fast. I said, "Bats sneak in the cracks at night and swirl around your head, and if they bite you, you need shots or you die. I've already had six shots and I'm only ten years old!"

"I'm eleven." He offered this fact as if it mattered.

I continued, "We hired thirty-two different bug spray guys, and they all left screaming. We've got *everything*. Bats, squirrels, ants, flies, moles. Centipedes and spiders, too. Sometimes snakes come right up the toilet! We save the spiders because they eat the other bugs."

He shrugged. "I ain't afraid of spiders or snakes."

My dad would split his pants over the word "ain't." He was a history teacher, but you'd think he taught English because of his obsession with words. But the school budget cut my dad, and words don't

4

worry him anymore. Just money. Right before we packed our summer stuff, my parents told us we had to sell the cabin. They couldn't afford a house, two cars, our cabin, and to still save college money for my sister, Amelia, and me.

I told the boy, "I'm not afraid of spiders, either. Even poisonous spiders. And I'm not afraid of snakes. I just don't like them."

The boy said, "I really don't have fears. Just born without them, I guess."

"You afraid of that house?" I pointed to the white two-story house where Mr. Edmund Clark lived, only a few hundred feet from our driveway. My parents made me say "mister" or "missus" when talking to old people, and Mr. Edmund Clark was old. He had a stiff leg and flabby face and silver hair like Olivia Stanger. He should probably have married Olivia Stanger since they were both mean and Mrs. Edmund Clark was dead.

Mud boy said, "Why would I be afraid of that house?"

"The guy there is mean and older than fossils."

His hands sprang to his hips. "That old guy is my grandpa."

"You mean your *grump*a?" I laughed, but he didn't.

Mud boy marched toward me with fists ready to spring. I karate kicked the air to show him I meant business. Then he laughed. "Do you know how stupid you look when you do that?"

"Do not!"

I held my arms ready to karate chop. He laughed even harder. He did this crazy spin-around karate kick with his arms waving. Then he stopped and held *his* arms ready to karate chop. We circled each other.

"I have a karate belt," he said.

"Me, too," I said.

"I also have a Judo belt," he said, circling some more.

I'd never heard of a Judo belt, but it sounded way better than a karate belt.

"Me, too," I said, circling some more.

"I punched gangster Al Capone in the stomach," he said.

"Me, too," I said. "Punched Al and his entire gang. Punched 'em all."

He stopped circling and stomped his foot. "Liar! Al Capone has been dead for like a hundred years! I know because he had a house down the road, and my grandpa's been there."

My lips sealed tight because I didn't know who Al Capone was or that he was dead or that Mr. Edmund Clark had been to his house.

Mud boy said, "I lied and said I punched him to prove *you* were lying." He sure looked proud of himself.

I'd been tricked. Now it was liar against liar. Because if the grump was his gramps, why hadn't I seen this kid before?

We stared at each other, karate-style. Judo-style.

Finally he said, "Your hair's really short for a girl."

That's what girls at school said—my hair's too

short and my clothes don't match. My cabin was supposed to be a fashion-free zone. "I don't have time for braids and ponytails. You got a problem with that?"

He thought about it. Then he dropped his karate arms. "I got a bucket of mud. I'm mixing up some mud pies."

"Mud pies?"

"Mud pies. Ten points for hitting that sign from here. Twenty bonus points for hitting her nose."

I was leading 80–40 when Dad shut down the contest. He looked at Olivia Stanger's face on that sign. Bits of grass clung to her silver waves, and her pretty violet-blue eyes were covered with mud. He shook his head and sighed.

Dad went into the cabin and came back with sponges and a bucket of soapy water. He set the bucket by our feet. "Looks like you and your friend have some work to do."

"If I ain't her friend, do I still have to clean this up?"

Ain't! Dad did not split his pants. He said, "Good question. Who are you?"

"Alex Clark."

"Ed's grandson?"

"And Neil and Sally Clark's son. We're buying the house and Grandpa's pizza restaurant so Grandpa can retire." Alex looked at me. "I can eat pizza anytime I want."

"Me, too," I said. "And brownies. Whenever I want."

Dad said, "No you can't, Christa. Now get busy."

We got busy, but I couldn't stop thinking about the stuff Dad and Mom were probably saying inside the cabin. I didn't even need to eavesdrop because I'd heard it all before.

Mom: *Christa, why can't you think before you act?*

Dad: *Christa, that's immature behavior.*

Mom: *Christa, you need to make better choices.*

Dad: *Christa, why can't you act your age?*

Someday I'll be sixteen like Amelia, and maybe then my parents will say things like, *I can't believe you're driving* and *our baby's growing up* and *you'll be graduating before we know it*. That's what they said to her. Seems like Amelia was always growing up too fast, and I was always growing up too slow. Too bad there wasn't a middle child who could've been just right.

When the sign was clean, Alex and I stood back and looked at our work.

"I liked it better before," he said.

Me, too. I scooped a glob of mud on my finger. Nobody was looking, far as I could tell. I rushed to the sign and did the job quick.

And there she was: cabin-thief Olivia Stanger. Big smile, front teeth blacked out.

CHASE TRUEGOOD AND THE NEW OLD AMELIA

Alex turned out to be the new version of the old Amelia, who used to play with me. It was his idea to meet the next day, but it was *my* idea to climb Mount Everest.

We met on the side of the hill by Mr. Edmund Clark's house. Alex sat in the grass and stuck out his foot.

"Do mine first," he said.

I took a fork and duct tape from my bag. I pressed the fork handle flat against the bottom of his shoe, leaving the tines sticking out past his toes. "Hold it," I said. While he held the fork in place, I tore off a long piece of duct tape and wrapped the fork tightly to his shoe.

"Presto!" I said. "Ice-climbing boots with spikes!"

I made his other shoe into spiked boots, and then he did mine.

A few years ago, Amelia and I had play-climbed Everest in a park near our house. That was when Amelia played with me. When Amelia was Pocahontas helping Lewis and Clark; I was Pocahontas's little sister. I was also the little sister of Sally Ride and Marie Curie and the people we invented, like adventurer Jade Truegood and her sister Chase.

But Amelia became a princess when she turned fourteen. One day, Amelia My Sister was plucking the legs off a daddy longlegs spider to see if it'd roll around with just a body. (Yes, it does.) Then practically overnight, Amelia My Sister vanished, and Amelia The Princess was in her place. Amelia The Princess screamed at bugs and begged for manicures and pierced ears.

I thought she'd be less royal at the cabin, but last summer she just watched movies and read romance novels and texted her friends. She'd sit on the dock and watch me swim—only because she wanted a tan—but she didn't play at all. My dad felt bad for me. He tried to play shipwreck and shark hunters, but he wasn't very good. It's not fun to play with someone who's constantly yelling, "Be careful!"

Fast-forward through the school year. Before we started packing for the cabin, Amelia made the biggest stink about leaving. She stomped around and cried about missing her friends and our parents ruining her life. I overheard the whole thing. She listed all the things she didn't want to do. She didn't want to swim or fish. She didn't want to look for night crawlers in the rain or have bonfires. Then she said it: "Another whole summer with just Christa? I'll go crazy!"

Dad told her she was a role model and that I looked up to her. I was too mad to listen. I went to my bedroom and punched my pillows.

Amelia was stupid. She had it backward! She

was going to drive *me* crazy with her hair tossing and lip glossing and the worst thing of all . . . her phone. Her stupid dumb stupid dumb dumb stupid stupid stupid stupid phone.

Who needed a sister? Not me.

Alex didn't have a phone for texting or long hair for tossing. Alex thought pretend-climbing Mount Everest was a brilliant way to spend a morning.

When I emptied out the bag on Mr. Edmund Clark's hill, Alex picked through the items with a smile on his face.

"Cassette tapes? Cool," he said. "My parents threw a bunch of these out when we moved."

I put one of the cassettes in my palm and spoke into it. " 'Roger that, base camp.' See? It's a walkie-talkie."

"And the oven mitts?"

"Climbing gloves. We don't keep winter stuff at the cabin, but these will work."

"Cool," he said.

And we were ready for Mount Everest.

CLIMBING THE DEADLY MOUNT EVEREST

The Adventure: The first kids to scale Mount Everest

The Place: Mount Everest (the big hill next to the Clarks' house)

The Characters: Chase Truegood (me) and Buck Punch (Alex)

The Wardrobe/Props: Oxygen masks (plastic cups with rubber bands), ice picks (forks and butter knives), boot spikes (forks duct-taped to shoe bottoms), mittens (oven mitts), walkie-talkies (Dad's old cassette tapes), and rope (rope)

Chase Truegood and Buck Punch have survived many adventures, but Mount Everest may be their last. Known as "killer mountain," Everest's steep cliffs and bottomless ravines lure climbers like buckets of worms lure fishermen.

Climbers rarely make it to the top. Chase's sister Jade, a once-famous mountain climber, failed to scale Mount Everest despite trying one hundred times.

The embarrassment forced her to retire. Luckily, Jade didn't die on the mountain like thousands of others—2,000 victims, to be exact. Might Chase and Buck bring the total to 2,002?

The team pulled themselves up a sheer wall of ice with handheld picks and spiked shoes, grunting and groaning from exhaustion.

"Urrbmph . . ." Buck could barely speak. "Radio base camp. Ask how much time before the blizzard hits." Talking nearly stole his last bit of energy. He breathed through the oxygen mask and spoke with a scratchy voice. "Chase, your tank's empty and mine's almost gone."

Chase mumbled into the walkie-talkie and repeated the news to Buck. "Base camp says we have two hours to reach Whitefish Peak and get back to camp. And the temperature has fallen to 300 below zero. Base camp says we must return now or die."

"We swore to do this or die trying. But maybe we should turn back," Buck said. Chase's neck was so cold she could barely nod. Buck held up his mitten-covered hands, using his last milligram of energy to shout, "My fingers . . . They're frozen!"

It turned out to be a near-fatal mistake. In lifting his hands, Buck dropped both of his handspikes, which he needed to pull himself to Whitefish Peak.

"Buck!" Chase shouted. "Hang on to the rope. Kick the ice 'til your boot spikes lock in. That'll hold you."

Buck tossed his oxygen tank to Chase. "You'll need this."

"No! We'll share it!" She spiked closer to Buck. The sideways-spike-lunge was the single most dangerous move in mountain climbing.

"Buck, we've climbed mountains without oxygen before," she said. "We will never ever give up. Never give up what's important to you, Buck! Never! Ever!"

"I broke my foot in the avalanche this morning. Didn't want to say," Buck gasped. He put the oxygen mask to Chase's nose while his eyes drooped shut. "Chase . . . go . . . on . . . without me."

"No!"

"I'm dying, Chase. Go . . . live our dream."

Buck flopped and then log-rolled down the ice, down where they'd escaped the avalanche, down into a dark hole.

Chase screamed.

"Christa Boyd-Adams! How many times do I have to shout?" Mom was standing by our picnic table near the cabin door. Her arms were crossed.

"WHAT? I CAN'T HEAR YOU!"

"Come home for lunch."

Mom always ruined fun with food. I yelled, "NOW?"

"Now!"

"I'M NOT HUNGRY."

"Stop shouting and get over here. I'm not telling you again."

"CAN ALEX EAT WITH US?"

"Christa, stop shouting and come here and talk to me."

I was just about to ask for ten more minutes

when Alex said, "We're having tacos like the ones you can buy in Arizona and chips and cookies."

"CAN I EAT WITH ALEX?"

"No. We're eating in town. Hurry up."

"FINE."

We scooted down the hill on our butts. I told Alex, "When I get back, we can go into the woods and climb my favorite tree."

"There weren't trees where I used to live," Alex said. "But my friends and I could climb a skyscraper if we wanted. I'm not afraid of heights at all."

I studied his face and said, "You're totally afraid of heights, aren't you?"

"Am not."

I heard a cough and a snort. Mr. Edmund Clark was walking slowly from the shore toward his shed. He had his fishing pole in one hand and a net in the other. It looked like he'd caught a couple of nice-sized perch. In all those years at our cabin, we'd only seen him fishing or working at his restaurant. Sometimes we'd be racing across the lake in our speedboat, and he'd be fishing from his boat in the cove at the lake's east side. Dad would slow down so our waves wouldn't interfere with his fishing. Mr. Edmund Clark did not like his boat to be rocked.

If he lived in a condo and made salad all day, I'd understand why he was an old crab. But he was surrounded by trees and water and pepperoni. How could someone with his own pizza business and a house on a lake—even if it was an old house—be so grumpy?

"Does he ever smile?"

Alex thought about it. "Dad told me not to expect hugs and kisses. He didn't say anything about smiles."

"My grandparents hug me all the time. They even hug Amelia."

"Until we moved here, I'd only seen my grandpa a few times."

That was strange. My grandparents lived in Florida, and we talked on the Internet every week and saw them at least four times a year—sometimes more! They gave me presents and candy and called me Angel, which made Amelia snort. By the looks of it, they were a lot younger than Alex's grandpa, too. His face was so wrinkly it made a raisin look like a grape! My grandma had just a few wrinkles, which she called "smile lines." If Mr. Edmund Clark hardly ever saw Alex, if he didn't have a grandchild for presents and hugs, then his wrinkles definitely weren't from smiles.

"Christa!" Mom's voice cut through the air. "I said now and I mean now!"

"COMING!"

When I stood up, my feet wouldn't bend because of the forks taped to my shoes. I had to keep my legs straight and wide, which made me walk like scissors. I could hear Alex laughing.

"What in the name of shoes are you doing?" Mr. Edmund Clark snapped at me.

I didn't answer, just scissored across the driveway as fast as I could.

PIZZA AND SUPERVISION

My family loved Clarks Pizza, the best restaurant in Hayward and in the world, actually. Amelia The Princess seemed to have forgotten that fact. She complained that pizza gave her pimples, but I figured Mr. Edmund Clark's pizza joint wasn't fancy enough for her. Nope. She probably wanted to eat at a fine-dining restaurant where the waiter put two forks by your plate in case you dropped one.

About a hundred years ago, Clarks Pizza had been one of those fancy places. Now the floors creaked under the waiters' feet, and water stains formed flat clouds on the ceiling. The restaurant still had a long wood bar with a mirror that stretched from one end to the other. The bar had shelves of old stuff, which Dad called artifacts. Sparkly crystal glasses, ladies' hats with feathers, the first-ever soda pop bottles, and flower-covered plates from the old restaurant. On the walls were black-and-white photos from the olden days and yellowed posters from the time when people wanted alcohol banned from the whole country. The posters looked like ink drawings and said things like "Alcohol Is Poison," "Safeguard the Babies: Parents Drinking Makes Weakly Children," and "Bootleggers and Their Booze Ruin Lives."

Every time we came for pizza, Dad read the menu's back flap and laughed. It said, *No! We don't sell alcoholic beverages. Get your beer somewhere else!*

My parents said the place was "charming" and "quaint"—they used those words a lot in the Northwoods—but the apostrophe made them crazy. The restaurant should be "Clarks' Pizza" or possibly "Clark's Pizza," but never "Clarks Pizza." And the menu said *beverages' come with free refills!* instead of *beverages come with free refills!* I learned more about apostrophes from Clarks Pizza than I did in school.

The only thing I cared about was the pizza. Mr. Edmund Clark put the *cheese* in the right place—all over the sauce in big mozzarella puddles. Delicious.

"Save room for dessert, because we're celebrating," Mom said.

I pumped my fist in the air. "We're not selling the cabin!"

"Honey, no. That's not what I meant. Still, it's good news. Dad and I have been hired to run a tutoring program here this summer. We'll be teaching!"

I was confused. "If you have jobs, why are we selling the cabin?"

"It's just temporary work, honey," Dad said. "The money will help, but it's not a permanent paycheck. This program runs for nine weeks."

"You're not going to have time to fish or swim or anything." I crossed my arms.

"We still have evenings and weekends."

"You have evenings and weekends during the school year, and all you do is grade papers and coach the stupid debate team!"

Dad shook his head. "It'll be different, honey. It's a summer program, and we won't be sending students home with a bunch of work. They do everything in class. We'll still have game night and bonfires. And we'll fish and swim. I promise." Dad nudged Amelia The Princess. "Tell Christa your news."

"It's so not a big deal, Dad." Amelia's fingers clicked on her phone while she talked. She didn't even look up. "But whatever. I'm going to be a waitress here. I get to use Mom's car." She grinned at the last part.

"For work only," Mom said. "Christa, listen up. Amelia will supervise while we're gone. Got it? No fighting. She's in charge."

Amelia looked so proud of herself. I pulled the paper from my straw down to the tip and blew from the other end. The paper hit Amelia's left eyebrow.

She frowned and mumbled, "I'm so sick of everyone letting you get away with murder."

"What happens when you're all working at the same time?" I asked. "Who's going to watch me then?"

Dad looked at Mom, and Mom cleared her throat. She looked at the table while she spoke. "The tutoring program is at the community center. So you could spend time in the library."

"The library? Are you kidding? That's like jail."

"There are other options," Dad said. "There's a summer rec program here, just like home. They have some fun classes." Only teachers would think the word "fun" belonged in front of the word "classes." Dad leaned forward and smiled at me. "They have a kids' taxidermy class."

"Really?" I wasn't expecting him to say that. Taxidermy? That might be worth a few afternoons at the community center.

"Gross!" Amelia wrinkled her nose. "Why would you want Christa to learn how to stuff dead animals? That's disgusting."

"Because Christa likes taxidermy," Mom said. "It's not disgusting. There's taxidermy on the walls everywhere up here. It's a hunting . . . art."

"I'm not blind, Mom. I know there's taxidermy everywhere up here. There's a deer head mounted in the ice cream shop for crying out loud."

They definitely had me at taxidermy, but then what? What came after taxidermy? I'd seen those summer rec catalogues, and I knew the other options would be horrible stuff like "Introduction to Beading" and "Create a Family Tree."

Amelia would not stop taxidermy bashing. "Christa and taxidermy? She'll want to save and mount every fish she catches and display them like school art projects. Our living room will be covered in sunfish. Next she'll be picking up dead raccoons from the road."

I sprinkled some Parmesan cheese on my palm and blew it in Amelia's face.

She shouted, "She got it in my eye!"

Mom grabbed the Parmesan jar from my hand. "Stop it. Both of you. I mean it."

I had to get away before I smacked Amelia and ended up grounded for the summer. I announced I was going to the bathroom, and Amelia said, "We'll weep the whole time you're gone."

That did it. I threw my napkin in her face and bolted out of the booth, yelling, "I hope your phone explodes!"

People turned and stared at us. I stomped across the restaurant and down the hall to the bathroom. I didn't have to go. I needed a few minutes for my parents to forget about that scene. I leaned against the wall by the ladies' room with my arms crossed.

Their news stunk more than Amelia's vanilla-spice-lavender-whatever body spray. The cabin was for sale, *and* my parents wouldn't have time to fish or play cards or do anything fun. It'd be just like home where all they did was grade papers and plan lessons. And I'd be stuck in stupid classes all day with adults telling me "wait your turn" and "pay attention" and "make better choices."

Farther down the hall I saw a handwritten sign stuck to the door by the kitchen. I knew it was the basement door because I'd seen Mr. Edmund Clark open it. I got closer so I could read it. The sign said:

KEEP OUT!
THERE IS NO LOOT UP HERE.
THERE IS NO LOOT DOWN THERE.
THERE IS NO LOOT ANYWHERE.
ENJOY YOUR PIZZA.

"I think it sounds like Dr. Seuss." A woman wearing a Clarks Pizza t-shirt (*Eatsa Some Pizza!*) studied the note. "Are you the girl who was playing in my yard this morning?"

She looked like Alex—brown eyes, dark skin, and a smile that seemed nervous.

"You're Alex's mom, right? I'm Christa."

"Sally Clark. You can call me Sally. My husband is Neil. We're running the restaurant now."

"What's the deal with this note?"

She shrugged. "Staff aren't supposed to be in the basement, and someone was rummaging around down there. Happens a lot, I guess."

"Rummaging for what?"

"Money. I didn't grow up here, but I'm told that Al Capone hid money in this area before he went to prison. Have you heard of Al Capone?"

"He's a gangster."

"A bootlegger," she said.

"That's a funny word."

She smiled. "It's what they call people who sold alcohol when it was illegal. Anyway, Al Capone had a place near here."

"A cabin. Alex told me."

She laughed. "Ed showed me photos of the place, and cabin isn't the right word. It's a beautiful stone house, and there's a separate bunkhouse and an eight-car garage and guard towers that protected the place from other gangs. There's a private lake, too."

"Al Capone had his own lake?"

"My husband says it was open for tours for many years. The owners built a restaurant and gift shop, but everything closed when the economy tanked."

"So why do people think there's loot at Clarks Pizza?"

"Rumors. People believe the craziest stories." She ran her hand over the sign, which was coming loose. She pressed it against the wood. "A real security system might help, but my father-in-law is too cheap and stubborn." Her face turned red. "I mean, he's careful with money and . . . he sticks by his decisions. I didn't mean cheap and stubborn." She cleared her throat. "Why don't you take me to your table? I want to meet your parents."

As soon as the introductions were made, Sally and my parents did that adult thing where they talked and talked like I wasn't even at the table. They talked about Neil managing a chain restaurant in Arizona and Neil not liking chain restaurants and about Mr. Edmund Clark's doctor telling him to retire and about Sally feeling excited for a real winter because she'd never touched snow, and it just got more boring. My stomach growled for pizza, and I wished Sally would go to the kitchen and find our food instead of chatting about snowflakes. I leaned closer to Amelia The Princess, who was huddling over her phone.

"Can I play a game on your phone?" I asked.

"I'm reading an article."

"What's the article about?"

She pressed the phone against her chest so I couldn't see. "It's about a ten-year-old girl who gets lost in the Northwoods of Wisconsin and a bear eats her."

I was going to kick her under the table and pretend it was an accident, but then I heard words coming together in a horrible way. Summer. Christa. Alex. Mr. Edmund Clark.

"He's watching Alex anyway," Sally said.

"But Ed's retiring," Dad said. "I don't want him to spend his summer watching Christa. His grandson is one thing, but toss in another kid? That doesn't seem right."

"Trust me, it'll be a lot less work for him if Alex has someone to play with. It'd be a huge favor to us if Christa could stay home with him."

Amelia's face curved into a huge smile, but my lips froze.

Mom squeezed my hand. "What do you think?

Would you like to stay with Mr. Clark while we work? You'd be on the lake instead of at the library. That'd be good, huh?"

Grumpy Mr. Edmund Clark in charge of me? All summer? Suddenly the library didn't sound so bad.

FINDERS KEEPERS AND LOSERS WEEPERS

Of all the vacation spots—mountains, parks, oceans, and canyons—the most beautiful place in the United States of America is Wisconsin's town of Hayward, definitely. The day before my parents' teaching program started, Dad and I took Alex on a tour to show him the town's best places.

We spent the morning at the National Fresh Water Fishing Hall of Fame, which is in a building shaped like a gigantic fish and obviously the best of all the halls of fame. Dad took pictures of us standing in the balcony, which is tucked inside the fish's mouth. We leaned on the fake fish teeth and smiled for the camera. After lunch, we watched a lumberjack demonstration and got ice cream from the world's best ice cream store. Then we went to the world's best candy store and watched the fudge lady, who worked in front of the window. She stirred fudge in a huge vat and smiled at the people on the sidewalk. I wondered if she ever stuck her finger in the vat and tasted the fudge when people weren't watching. The fudge lady had the best job in the world.

But I saved the best for last. While Dad went to the used bookstore, I took Alex around the corner and down two blocks to Nan's Bait and Tackle.

We always got our live bait from Nancy "Nan" Kline, who opened her very own bait store when she graduated high school. She'd been selling bait and tackle for more than thirty years. I wanted to become Nan's partner when I finished school. Every time I left the store she'd tell me, "Hurry up and graduate, would ya?" As far as I was concerned, Nan was the only person who could tell me to grow up.

Alex gagged when I opened the door. He spit his candy into the trash can and plugged his nose.

"Man, it stinks! The smell is making my sour worms taste like fish."

I looked around. Nan wasn't at the counter, so she was probably in the back room. I hissed, "That's mean! Don't let her see you plugging your nose."

Alex's arms dropped to his sides, but the frown didn't leave his face. "I don't see what's so special about this place."

True, the floor was dirty. Paint peeled from the walls near the ceiling. Everything that had once been white was now gray. It looked exactly like it should—like a place where Hayward's most expert fishermen and fisherwomen swapped stories about the ones that got away.

I pulled Alex by the arm and led him to the bait tanks that lined the wall. A kid from Arizona had a lot to learn about living on a lake.

"I'll teach you about the different kinds of bait."

"I don't need you to teach me."

"These are golden shiners. They're great for catching big fish. Have you ever used golden shiners?"

Alex watched the minnows dart across the tank. He moved to the next tank and then the next. "I like these silver ones better."

"Fathead minnows? They're very ordinary."

Clearly Mr. Edmund Clark hadn't explained bait to his only grandson. Weird. The old man wasn't a chit-chatter, but he could talk bait and tackle forever. He once spent ten minutes by the dock—in the pouring rain—telling my dad that walleyes bit on fatheads and chub in the spring, but you definitely want to switch to worms and leeches in the summer. Dad was wet and freezing but didn't leave until the lecture was done because Mr. Edmund Clark is so scary.

"Look who's here! Christa Boyd-Adams." Nan's arms squeezed me from behind. I turned and hugged her back. She'd cut her long red hair into a short bob, but she still smelled like bait and earth and pine. Northwoods perfume. "I was wondering when you'd stop in."

"My parents sold our boat, but we're still going to fish from the dock."

"I saw your mom a few days ago. She told me about the boat and selling the cabin. I'm sorry." She mussed up my hair. "I'm selling the shop, too, so we'll go out at the same time. Seems right, doesn't it?"

"What? Why?" I nearly dropped my bag of candy. "That's crazy!"

"Tough business, selling bait and gear. One of the new gas stations started selling bait, plus someone's opening a shop in that new strip mall. Besides, a young couple wants to buy the building. Good timing for me."

Alex wandered down the wall of tanks, watching the minnows. Olivia Stanger was selling his neighbor's cabin, the bait shop was closing, and his grandfather wasn't making pizza anymore. He didn't even care.

Nan said, "You'll get a chuckle out of this. The buyers want to remodel my building and open a tea shop." She faked a British accent. "They will sell the finest English tea and crumpets."

"That's the dumbest thing I've ever heard!"

Nan laughed as she wandered back to the register and poured herself coffee from the little pot on the counter. "Funny thing, isn't it? Tourists leave the suburbs and come to our little town to get *away* from the suburbs, and what do they want? Stuff from the suburbs."

Nan was not getting a chuckle out of me because it wasn't funny. How could everything change in one summer? And all because of money.

The door opened and a police officer stepped inside. "Sheriff Duncan! How are you?" Nan poured him a cup of coffee, and they started that adult talking-about-the-weather thing.

I looked at the fishing pole display with Alex until he nudged me and pointed to the register where Nan and the sheriff stood. I heard the words "trespassing" and "vandalism."

"The last bunch just dug holes in the ground, like they figured money had been buried. All this nonsense is happening in my county, on my watch. I've had it. So I'm just wondering if any tourists have been asking for directions to Capone's property." The sheriff's voice was deep as a tuba. He towered over Nan, and his eyes looked like ice. When he yelled *halt*, I bet people halted.

"Not that I remember," Nan said. "Why tourists?"

"Well, I got to thinking that the trespassers might not be local. Maybe some of the tourists have been asking questions about how to get there and what the security is like. That kind of thing."

"Nope. The only thing tourists ask me about is the best fishing spots." She refilled his coffee. "I wish someone would buy Capone's old property from the bank and reopen it. How'd a treasure like that go bankrupt in the first place? Even my tiny bait shop survived the recession."

"Advertising," Sheriff Duncan said. "I don't think they did enough advertising."

Amelia The Princess was always telling me to mind my own business, but some people's business was just too interesting. I left Alex by the display, walked to the counter, and butted into their conversation. "Nan, has anyone ever found any money out there? Or anywhere?"

She leaned on the counter. "In the 1970s, an old guy named Sherwin Johnson was remodeling a resort Capone's buddies stayed at years ago. He opened up a wall and found a few thousand dollars."

"Serious?" My voice squeaked with excitement.

"Dead serious."

"Did he get to keep it?"

"I suppose so," Nan said. "Nobody could put a real claim on it, could they? All those gangsters were dead."

I nodded. "Finders keepers."

Sheriff Duncan took a sip of his coffee and looked right in my eyes. "The problem, young lady, is that whenever you have finders keepers, you also have losers weepers. That's what makes it a crime."

"Someone was digging around at Clarks Pizza, too. They broke into the basement." I looked at Alex, thinking he'd speak up, but he just stared at his shoes.

Sheriff Duncan didn't look surprised, "Well, now, that's different. Sherwin Johnson stumbled upon the money. He had no connection. The Clarks were actual business associates of Capone's. Crooks, all of them. The son left town and never came back. Don't tell me that's not suspicious."

Alex's cheeks went white to red, like his whole face had been pinched.

Nan said, "I went to school with Neil. He was a good guy. The Clarks never had two dimes to rub together. They aren't sitting on a fortune."

"Course they are," Sheriff Duncan said. "That's why Neil ran off. He's mad because old Ed wants to donate his stash to the fishing hall of fame. Everyone says so. That guy's nuttier than a peanut factory."

"Ed was never the same after Mrs. Clark died. He made Neil quit the hockey team because he needed him to work in the restaurant. Neil could've had a scholarship. He was that good. Anyway, he left because he wanted a new life. It didn't have anything to do with money." Nan smiled. "Neil was a cutie."

This had turned into an awkward moment, for sure. Normally I barely noticed awkward moments— my parents were always explaining them to me afterward—but this made me want to crawl out of my skin. I had to stop this before poor Alex melted into the floor. I cleared my throat and said, "This is Alex Clark, Neil's son. They moved here to take over the restaurant."

Nan's face went white-red even faster than Alex's, but Sheriff Duncan just cocked his head. "You don't say."

"I do say. They moved here from Arizona."

Sheriff Duncan studied Alex from head to toe. Finally he said, "Welcome to Hayward, Alex Clark."

Nan stammered. "So . . . Alex Clark. Neil's son." Then she thought a moment. "You're Neil's *son?* Goodness, he got a late start. I already have two grandsons your age."

"Oh." Alex rocked on his feet a bit.

"Well, you better be on your way, Christa," Nan said. "And Alex, tell your dad I said hello. Seems like I'm always open, so tell him to stop by, okay?"

"By all means," Sheriff Duncan said. "I'm always open, too. Tell him to stop by."

THE CANOE AND THE BASEMENT

DISCOVERING TREASURE IN A SHIPWRECK

The Adventure: Searching for Buck Punch's family fortune

The Place: Whitefish Island, Pacific Ocean (Mr. Edmund Clark's sunken canoe, Whitefish Lake)

The Characters: Chase Truegood (me) and Buck Punch (Alex)

The Wardrobe/Props: Scuba suits (swim suits with life jackets), oxygen tanks (thermoses held in place with a belt), Exploration Collectron tools (coffee mugs, forks, spoons, salad tongs), swim goggles (swim goggles), and rope (rope)

Chase Truegood and Buck Punch have survived many adventures, but searching for Captain Capone's lost treasure might be their last.

A year before, infamous pirate Captain Capone stole Buck's family fortune and kidnapped Chase's sister Jade. Capone's ship disappeared in the fog and shark-filled waters by Whitefish Island. The ship has never been found. Until now. By treasure hunters Chase Truegood and Buck Punch.

Buck, with the survivor rope around his wrist, jumped into the thrashing waves from the dock of their explorer ship. Chase tightened her goggles and pressed her face into the water to watch for deadly sharks. When Chase felt a tug, she pulled the rope with all her might until Buck popped from the water.

He coughed up seawater and said, "It's definitely Captain Capone's ship. Says so right on the side. Good thing my goggles have lights." Buck emptied rocks from the Exploration Collectron mug next to Chase.

Chase inspected Buck's samples with the Exploration Collectron spoon. "This stone is from the necklace Jade was wearing when she was kidnapped. Do you think she survived the shipwreck?"

"Depends. Was she a good swimmer?"

"A long time ago, she was the fastest," Chase said. "Then she got slow and turned afraid and retired."

Buck nodded. "The sharks are thick down there. Maybe they ate her." He straightened his goggles. "I'm going back down to look for my family's fortune."

"I better go, too, Buck. It's almost feeding time for the sharks. Two people oughta be down there."

"You stay here. I don't need back-up."

"I'll be the front-up. You be the back-up."

"Chase, I'm the faster swimmer. I'll be the front-up."

Chase wondered if Buck's concussion from his earlier dive was making him crazy. Everyone knew she'd won the international swimming race three years in a row. Despite his very best try, Buck came in last place.

"We'll dive together!" Chase said. "We can't take chances. We need that money in case Captain Capone is holding my sister hostage and wants a ransom."

"Yes! I'll give you my money."

"You're the best partner ever, Buck!"

Buck and Chase dove into the dark waves and blasted to the ocean floor at top speed. They pulled themselves around the ship, sticking their hands in every hole, feeling around for gold and silver.

Buck grabbed Chase's arm. Having been trained in sign language, he signed a message to Chase. "Look out! Sharks!"

"Hide in the ship!" Chase signed back with scared fingers.

Before Buck could answer, his whole body jerked. Chomped! Buck was chomped by a shark! Chase remembered the bottle of shark repellent in her scuba suit pocket. As she sprayed the shark's face,

Chase pulled Buck to the surface. They had barely climbed onto their explorer boat when the shark torpedoed out of the water, narrowly missing Chase's head.

"He got me, Chase." Buck rolled in pain.

"Thank God it's only a scratch."

"Yes, a scratch. But sharks at Whitefish Island have poison on their fins. It finned me, Chase."

Buck's eyelashes fluttered, then closed.

"Buck! Hang on. I've got the anti-fin medicine in the starbird engine."

He moaned. "Too . . . late . . . Go on without me, Chase." Now he wheezed. "Find the treasure . . . Save . . . your . . . sister."

"We find the fortune together, or we don't find it at all!" Chase screamed.

"Chase Truegood, turn down the volume, will ya?" Amelia stood on the dock, hands on her hips, showing off her uniform: jean shorts and an *Eatsa Some Pizza* t-shirt. "I'm going to work, and you

49

guys are being called for lunch. A storm's coming, so your next bold adventure might be a card game."

Clouds were collecting in the sky, gathering in gray clumps.

Amelia The Princess stared into the water. "Is that a canoe?"

I shrugged.

"Really? You guys sunk a canoe? Alex?"

"I think it was an accident," he said.

"It was not an accident," Amelia said. "Why'd you do that?"

I took off my goggles so I could see her better. "We needed a shipwreck. It's not easy to sink a canoe. Trust me. Alex had to pour water into it while I jumped up and down. I fell like twenty times." This information would have impressed Amelia My Sister.

"That's correct. It is not easy to sink a canoe. You know why?" She paused, but neither of us answered. "Because canoes float! Where is Mr. Clark? Are you supposed to be down here without supervision?"

"Do you want to play when you get home?" I asked.

"Christa, I asked you a question. Are you supposed to be down here without supervision?"

Alex said, "Grandpa said it's okay as long as we're wearing life jackets."

"Do you?" I asked. "This canoe is awesome. Come on. It'll be fun!"

She shook her head and stomped to Mom's car without a word.

Alex pulled himself onto the dock and unclipped his life jacket. "You think we're gonna be in trouble?" He wiped his face on his towel, which was so dirty it left brown streaks on his face.

I crossed my fingers behind my back and said, "It's a boat. Water can't hurt it, Alex."

Cheese sandwiches were already on the table with cans of orange soda and potato chips. This was our first lunch with Mr. Edmund Clark, and we were off to a good start. No tuna, no carrots, no raisins or apple slices. He understood potato chips came from vegetables, luckily.

The air was heavy and thunder grumbled. I loved storms because they gave the woods a bath, and everything smelled pure. I poked Alex. "You know why it smells good after it rains?"

"Because your nose sensors need cleaning." He said this all confident, like he'd learned it at school.

I laughed. "That's just stupid! You wouldn't know about rain because you're from Arizona. Rain smells nice because it kicks up bacteria from the ground, and the bacteria smell good, kind of sweet, actually."

"Now that's stupid." He picked the crust from his sandwich without breaking it, leaving a perfect square on his plate.

"My mom's a science teacher. She told me."

"Dough smells good because water kicks the yeast around, and it makes the smell of dough. My family's pizza is so good because we got the recipe from Italian people in Chicago."

I'd been wanting to ask Alex about his family and gangsters since our visit to the bait shop. This was my chance. "Were the Italian people gang-sters?"

Alex chewed fast and hard. "I don't know. Who cares? That was like a hundred years ago. If my family knew gangsters, they were probably trying to reform them."

"Maybe that's why your grandpa wants to donate all the gangster money to the National Fresh Water Fishing Hall of Fame. He wants to do something good with bad money."

"There isn't any gangster money!" Potato chip crumbs flew from his mouth as he talked. "I asked my dad about everything the sheriff said at the bait shop. My dad said small towns are rumor mills, and that's partly why he left. He said everything started from one stupid picture. One night Al Capone ate dinner at Clarks Fine Dining, and my great grandpa asked if they could get a picture taken together because Capone was famous. So they did, and my great grandpa hung it on the wall. That was it. He served Capone a steak, and they took a picture."

"Did you ask your grandpa about it?"

"I asked my dad. Why would I ask my grandpa?"

"Your dad wasn't even born then. Your grandpa is closer to the real story."

"I just told you the real story."

"Then why do people keep rummaging around the basement of the restaurant?"

He kept me waiting while he chugged his soda. "Because people here are stupid."

I couldn't believe those words came from his mouth. I wanted to throw potato chips at him, but I was too afraid of Mr. Edmund Clark. I slipped my hands between my legs and the chair so I wouldn't use them for trouble. "You get to live here and you don't even know how lucky you are!"

"Why do you like it here so much?"

"Because it's awesome!"

"What's so awesome about it? I don't see anything awesome."

"If it wasn't thundering, we could play in the rain. Playing in the rain is awesome."

Alex brought his plate to the sink and sort of

slammed it against the counter. He stood in front of the window, his back to me, watching the rain hammer the earth. Even if I tried to explain, he wouldn't get it because he loved Arizona and probably had a hundred friends there and probably never got in trouble at school.

I loved the Northwoods for so many reasons. At the cabin my parents belonged to me instead of their students. There weren't any girls at Whitefish Lake telling me my clothes didn't match or that my hair looked funny. In school, I had to sit on my hands to keep them from causing trouble. My hands could do anything at the cabin because they didn't have to be wrapped around a stupid pencil. And for a long time, I had the world's best cabin friend. Amelia My Sister.

Alex shoved his fists in his pockets. "I don't like the rain, and my dad says it rains half the summer. Dad likes it dry. He doesn't like ice or snow or rain or lakes or pine trees."

"Why'd he come back if he hates it so much?"

"Grandpa's old and sick, and my grandma's been

dead since my dad was a kid, so I guess Grandpa's pretty lonely. Mom wants them to make peace. And Dad thought it'd be good to own a restaurant instead of work for someone who owns a restaurant."

"Trust me, he picked a good place to own a restaurant, even if it rains. Even if it gets cold. The cold is amazing, actually. If you cry outside in the winter, your eyes actually freeze shut. Where else does something like that happen?"

"You'd have to be a crybaby to freeze your eyes shut."

Alex picked a stray potato chip off the floor and ate it, like it was no big deal that it'd been on the dirty floor. Just chewed and swallowed without even shouting, "Five-second rule!" I liked Alex, even if he was confused about Wisconsin. I wanted this almost-argument to end, so I didn't let myself get mad about the crybaby thing.

"Sometimes I get the eye sweats when I'm sad, but that's not *crying*." I said it all calm.

"I didn't get eye sweats when I left my friends in Arizona, but they did. All of them. It was like an army of friends with sweaty eyes."

Alex was lucky to have an army of friends to miss. I didn't have an army. The girls in my class didn't invite me to parties or sleepovers because I don't like dolls, jewelry-making kits, crafts, hair braiding, cookie baking, dancing, gymnastics, reading, cute clothes, or sparkle shoes. Those girls said my pretend-play is weird. At home I only had my neighbor Danny Kellerman. He liked making up stories, but he was only eight, and he spent summer in daycare. Plus he whined too much. Alex was way better than Danny Kellerman.

"So what should we do until the storm stops?" I asked.

"You better think of something because you can't pester me all day." The voice came from Mr. Edmund Clark, and I almost jumped out of my chair. He'd wandered into the kitchen for some water. I thought the kitchen must be as old as

Mr. Edmund Clark. Someone had painted the cupboards white, but the paint bubbled and peeled. You could see dirt around the handles, too. The beige countertop was stained, and the floor was sticky. He should've been spending the gangster money on a new kitchen, or at least a cleaning lady.

Alex asked, "When it stops raining, would you take us out in the boat? Maybe tubing?"

"Tubing? You can barely swim thanks to living in a state drier than the moon. Ari*stona*. Good lord. It should be a prison colony."

"I can float. Besides, I'll wear a life jacket."

Mr. Edmund Clark said something that sounded like *no* just as thunder shook the house. Then he wiped his mouth with his sleeve and shook his head. "Damn thunderstorm. What am I going to do with you two?"

Alex asked, "You wanna watch a movie, Christa?"

Mr. Edmund Clark grumped. "Don't be getting any ideas about changing up my television programs. You can run around the basement. But don't touch my taxidermy or my tools."

I had no idea Mr. Edmund Clark was an artist. That made him a little less scary. I so wanted to touch his taxidermy stuff.

Alex said to me, "One of his squirrels is posed like a ballet dancer spinning on one foot. It's like something from a scary movie."

"It's funny! Don't you know funny when you see it?" Mr. Edmund Clark slapped his hand on the table. "I'm building a collection for you and your father, so you have something to remember me by after I croak."

"Do we really have to play in the basement?" Alex asked.

"Something wrong with the basement? It's an indoor playground."

"It's . . . dark," Alex said. "That one stuffed raccoon doesn't have any eyes. It's old and scary down there."

"Basements don't scare me," I said.

"Me, either," Alex said. "I was just thinking of you."

Mr. Edmund Clark's voice boomed with the thunder. "I'm old and scary! Ain't nothing wrong with old and scary." He got quiet, and he leaned closer to us and said, "BOO!"

We screamed. He laughed and laughed.

ZANIMALS AND
THE PIPE

ESCAPING A DANGEROUS
UNDERGROUND PIT

The Adventure: Escaping an underground pit after being captured by Al Capone

The Place: A secret underground pit (Mr. Edmund Clark's basement)

The Characters: Chase Truegood (me) and Buck Punch (Alex)

The Wardrobe/Props: Ladder (ladder), washtub

(washtub), hammer (hammer), flashlights (flashlights), and rope (rope)

Chase Truegood and Buck Punch have survived many adventures, but being held hostage by Al Capone in an underground pit might be their last.

As the team chased Capone and his crooks, the tables turned and Capone and his crooks captured Chase and Buck. The bad guys threw them into an underground pit that nobody could ever find.

Chase pounded on the walls. "Nothing's hollow. The pit's surrounded by rock."

Buck was all nervous. "We ain't got much battery power in these flashlights. When they go out, it'll be—"

"Pure black." Chase finished his sentence. "We'll be blind, and nobody will ever find us."

"Maybe the police will look here when we're reported missing. I have to get back to my team of detectives in Arizona. I have to!"

"The police won't help. They're working with Capone!"

"Maybe your sister Jade will come out of retirement and—"

"Jade is a coward!" Chase shouted.

The pit was full of junk. Attached to the wall was a dirty old washtub with a faucet, so at least they wouldn't die from thirst. Old boxes and stuff covered the floor, and a workbench displayed the ugliest taxidermied animals in the history of taxidermy—two raccoons, two squirrels, a fox, and a bobcat—all misshapen and put in weird poses. The raccoon's legs were turned the wrong way, and one of the squirrels held the shape of a ballet dancer standing on one foot, its other leg pointing straight to the side.

Suddenly, the furry creatures came to life. Zombie animals, aka zanimals! The zanimals inched toward them, growling and hissing.

"What?" Buck asked when he noticed Chase's face.

Chase pointed and yelled, "The stuffed animals are coming to life! Look! Zanimals!"

Buck waved his flashlight, which revealed even more deadly zanimals. "They have poison teeth like

63

the Arizona zanimals, which are the world's most dangerous zanimals."

"The Arizona zaminals were recently replaced by the Wisconsin zanimals as the world's most dangerous. But I don't have time to explain it to you, Buck. I can see the venom dripping from their mouths!"

Buck pulled a ladder from the junk, steadied it on the floor, and pointed at the ceiling. "We might have an escape route."

The ceiling was made of wood—not stone—but it had thin orange pipes among the boards. "I've got the hammer," Chase said. "We'll break the wood and squeeze between those pipes. Hurry!"

Chase and Buck took careful steps up the ladder so they wouldn't fall to the floor and become food for the coming-to-life zanimals. The eyeless raccoon ran into a wall, but the bobcat was getting close.

"You stay on this step and kick 'em away," Chase said. "I'm climbing to the top even though there's a sticker on this ladder that says, 'Do not stand on top step.'" Chase pulled a hammer from her back pocket.

"Hurry Chase. I . . . I . . ."

"What?"

"I got bit on my ankle while I was kicking the zanimals."

"Hold on. I'll pound our way out of here, and we'll race to town and get the anti-venom."

The ladder shuddered with both of their weight. Chase had one last step to climb before she was on the very top. "Keep the ladder steady."

"I'm tryin', Chase, I'm tryin'. I'm feeling a little weak and a little blind, and my foot swelled up and popped my shoe off. The only people who could save me now live thousands of miles away in Arizona."

"They ran off with Jade, Buck. I'll save you!" Chase hammered on the ceiling, listening for something that sounded hollow. The ladder swayed. Both of them tried to hold steady, but the ladder tipped. Just as Chase was about to fall to the ground, she grabbed the orange pipe on the ceiling and clung to it, like a child on monkey bars.

Chase screamed. The ladder crashed into the washtub, which came loose and nearly fell off the wall. Chase held tight to the orange pipe. Buck rolled on the floor, groaning.

A split second of silence. Then the pipe snapped in half, dropping Chase to the ground. Water burst from the pipe and sprayed the concrete floor.

And that's what happened. For real. Not the zanimals, but everything else: the falling ladder, the broken washtub, the exploding pipe, Alex and I crumpled on the floor.

Shock kept away the pain. Alex was so stunned, his pupils shrunk into the white space around his eyes. I grabbed his arm. "Are we in trouble?"

Now that was a dumb question. The door opened and Mr. Edmund Clark hollered, "What's going on down there?"

For an old guy, Mr. Edmund Clark came downstairs fast. Rocket fast. He saw water spraying from the cracked pipe and shouted, "The water main! Turn it off! Get off your butts and turn it off!"

I had no idea what a water main was, or how to turn it off. Alex and I stayed on our butts, too shocked to move. I wanted to shrink into the floor and turn into a zanimal, which didn't seem like such a bad life, really. Much better than being a kid who snapped a water pipe in two.

"For the love of Gertrude!" Mr. Edmund Clark marched around the stairs to the other side of the basement. I couldn't see him, but I heard him grump and groan. The spray turned into a few sprinkles, then stopped. I belly crawled to the washtub and tried to hide underneath, but I was too big and the tub's edge was practically touching the floor.

Squishy footsteps came closer. *Squish. Squish. Squish.* I peeked and saw Alex huddled against the wall. A very wet Mr. Edmund Clark sat down on a wood box next to Alex. He coughed and caught his breath before speaking.

"Alex, your mother doesn't like shouting or

cussing, and one must respect rules set down by the lady of the house. So with all due respect to your mother," his voice rose from its quiet place, "what in the unholy firestorms of hell were you doing?"

I faced the wall, waiting for Alex to answer. That's when I noticed a hole about the size of a watermelon. Where the washtub had been hanging was an open space in the basement's wall. I wished that hole were big enough to hide a ten-year-old girl.

"We . . . we . . . were climbing on the ladder because of the zombie animals, and we were gonna pound our way through the ceiling to escape the crooks. And the ladder crashed. And Chase—I mean Christa—held on to the pipe to *save her life*. To save her life! And the pipe broke."

"I better be going deaf, because if you just said something about my art and crooks and zombies, then your brain needs a good cleaning."

Even though we were in big-time trouble, I couldn't stop looking at that hole. Could anyone resist looking in a hole? Not me. I put my hand inside it and felt around until I found two pieces of paper. I shook off the dirt and looked close. I shouted before Mr. Edmund Clark's voice geared up for a good, long yell.

"Two hundred dollars!"

"Oh, it'll cost more than that to fix this mess—"

"Money!" I yelled, crawling out of my hiding space and waving the two bills in the air. The bills were soggy and smelled like wet socks.

They leaned toward me, and Mr. Edmund Clark took the money from my hand. He tilted his head to look under the sink. His face didn't change expression, but Alex's mouth dropped open.

Mr. Edmund Clark stared at the money and said, "Hell's bells. How'd this get left behind? Anything else in that hole?"

"Not that I could tell," I said.

His eyes, his whole body, seemed to float away, maybe into a memory. He whispered, "This was supposed to be gone a long time ago. Cleaned out and . . . gone. Burned."

I thought maybe he'd lost his mind a little.

"Gone? Was there more money?" Alex asked.

"Enough to fill a suitcase, but . . . I had no idea she hid it here. Maybe she hid it here and then burned it."

"Who?" I asked.

"My mother," he said. "She called it blood money. She said it was cursed."

"There's more?" Alex said. "Where is it?"

Grumpa patted Alex's leg, and his voice got loud again. "Well, looks like you and the Tomboy of Terror just uncovered traces of the family loot."

Neil was wrong. The sheriff was right. The Clarks had gangster money, a suitcase full of it. And if my neighbors had enough money to fill a suitcase, then maybe there was enough to save a cabin.

Alex and I rocked on the front porch swing after the storm. We hoped his grandpa would tell us about the Clark family loot, but he made us sit on the swing so we couldn't "destroy the house." Then he got on the phone, calling a buddy to bring tools and help fix the pipe.

So we swung and waited and talked about the money. Where'd they get it? Was it from bootlegging? How much money would fit in a suitcase? Why'd Alex's great-grandmother hide money in a wall if she wanted to burn it? It was a mystery.

"Alex, why'd your great-grandmother put money in a wall instead of a bank?"

"It was the olden days. They probably didn't have banks."

"Banks invented money, Alex! That's why people say money doesn't grow on trees. Because it was invented by banks."

"I knew that. Just forgot." He picked at the rubber peeling off the bottom of his shoe. "I guess my family had too much money. The bank didn't have enough space."

That about burned me up. *Too much money.* Nobody said those words in my house. Just words about bills. Car bills and credit card bills and house bills. My parents also talked all the time about the school's bills. The school had no money, just bills so big they had to budget cut my dad. What if they budget cut my mom, too? What if we lost our cabin and our cars and our house? I hated bills.

A car turned into the driveway and pulled up to the house. This old guy got out. He didn't have hair on his head, but his face was covered with gray whiskers. He smiled at us, but it was a creepy smile with crooked teeth. Mr. Edmund Clark stepped onto the porch and said, "Walt Miller!"

"At your service, Ed. With tools." Mr. Walt Miller gave a salute and flashed his crooked teeth some more.

"Took you long enough. I was beginning to think you had to fly to Detroit for those tools."

Mr. Walt Miller shook his head. "Duncan pulled me over because of my brake lights. Guess they went out. That man should be in town protecting businesses instead of wandering county roads, bothering folks who live here."

"Fix your brake lights."

"Duncan says there's been more trouble out at Capone's hideout. He's keeping his eye on the place." Walt shook his head and muttered, "Duncan needs better eyes."

"You drove by Capone's? That's the long way here."

"Just trying to get around the tourist traffic."

I wanted to ask about the trouble at Capone's property, but Mr. Edmund Clark was glaring at us. He whispered, "Don't say anything about that hole or the money. I don't need any gossip. I braced the washtub so it covers the hole. Not a word to anybody."

His words made me forget about bills. If he didn't want anyone to know, then he wouldn't tell my parents about me flooding his basement. Saved from grounding! That gave me happy tingles.

Mr. Walt Miller walked up the porch steps and looked at us. "Guess you kids just learned the difference between copper pipes and monkey bars."

Mr. Edmund Clark shook his head. He squinted at me. "Christa. That name's a bit too sweet, and you're one slippery kid. I think I'm gonna call you Minnow."

"I always wanted a nickname." My face beamed. "And you can have a nickname, too, because Mr. Edmund Clark is too long. I think I'm gonna call you Grumpa."

He opened the front door and let it slam behind him and his buddy. But he didn't say no.

THE CANOE (AGAIN) AND GAME NIGHT

It is not easy to unsink a canoe.

And it is not easy to explain why the canoe has been sunk and why you didn't mention it right away and why you didn't respect property belonging to someone else.

When a canoe is under water, it's very, very heavy. The sand doesn't want to give it up. Dad, Neil, Mom, and even Amelia grunted and groaned in chest-high water, lifting and pushing and pulling the canoe back to shore. It was so heavy Amelia invited her new friend Matt to help. He worked with her at the restaurant, and I could tell immediately that he wasn't just a friend but a potential prince, because she was laughing and smiling.

Grumpa watched from the dock with his arms crossed. Alex kicked rocks on the shore and looked sorry while I used a stick to draw dollar signs in the sand. He whispered to me, "I never got in trouble with my friends in Arizona."

I kicked sand at him when the canoe-savers weren't watching. When they were watching, I tried to look sorry. Very, very sorry.

Alex and I wanted to hear Grumpa's story about the hole and the money, but Amelia ratted us out first. Mr. Walt Miller had left, our parents had come home, and everyone had rushed to the lake all worried, like a mermaid had washed up on shore or something. Such a big deal over a dumb canoe.

Alex's mom Sally walked down the slope toward the shore. She mussed Alex's hair and said, "Tell me you've run out of trouble, kiddo. Tell me your tank's empty."

"Yeah, it's empty. Sorry, Mom."

She pulled off her sandals. "I should get in the water."

"Don't. Christa and I should help." Alex called, "We'll help."

Our dads yelled *no* at the same time.

So we waited. I wondered about everything, but I hid my wondering under my sorry face. I wondered about the Clarks' money. I wondered about Mr. Walt Miller and Sheriff Duncan and the trouble at Al Capone's old house. I wondered why people would stuff money in a wall and why Grumpa would keep it a secret from his buddy Mr. Walt Miller. I wondered how money could just float around the universe and not land in the laps of nice people, people who had important things to save.

Finally, the canoe made it to shore. They tipped it on its side to dump out the water and pushed it into the weeds. "Well, that's enough fun for to-night," Neil said. "Let's go have dinner."

"That's it?" Grumpa grumped. "That's all you're going to say to these kids?"

"What do you want me to do? Make them wash dishes at the restaurant for a week? Maybe you should be watching them instead of TV." Neil's voice sounded like a snap: quick and sharp.

Grumpa shoved his fists in his pockets and stared at Neil, who stared back. Alex stopped kicking rocks, but he didn't look at me or them or anyone. The only sound was the buzz from a Jet Ski on the other side of the lake. Dad cleared his throat and said, "Okay then. Well . . . enjoy your dinner. We're having game night, so . . . we'll be heading inside, too."

Matt the waiter helped save the canoe, but he ruined game night. He bugged me. He was like a fly buzzing around your face while you're eating an ice cream cone. Matt laughed at everything my parents said—proof he was a liar because my parents weren't funny.

Matt didn't know how to play gin rummy so we couldn't play gin rummy. Matt didn't know how to play canasta so we couldn't play canasta. We had to play Monopoly. Matt got Boardwalk *and* Park Place, which he sold to Amelia because she smiled and tossed her hair. He didn't even ask for a profit.

No, I didn't like him, even his name. Matt. Matt. Matt. Cat. Bat. Hat. Fat. Pat. Vat. That. Drat. Brat. Nobody's name should rhyme with that many words.

Amelia said, "We should have a bonfire night." It was shocking—Amelia The Princess wanted to leave the castle and venture into her kingdom!

"It's supposed to rain." Mom looked out the window over the sink. "It's sprinkling already."

Matt said, "I can make popcorn. Real popcorn, the kind on the stove, not from the microwave. Do you have any kernels? I'll make some."

"We do," Dad said. "We tried to make real popcorn over a campfire last year. *Tried*. We burned it and ended up eating microwave popcorn around the fire."

Everyone laughed except me.

Mom and Matt dug through the cupboards for a pan and oil and popcorn. Amelia watched them all happy. She wasn't even holding her texting machine. Dad squeezed my knee and leaned close. "What's up, sweetie? You're so quiet."

I whispered, "He's ruining game night."

"How?"

"Because it's supposed to be just us, and this might be our last game night ever!" My voice shook, and I could feel my eyes start to sweat.

"We'll always have family game night, no matter where we are. You have to stop confusing the place with the people. Our family is important. Not the cabin."

I wanted to wrestle Dad to the ground until he took his stupid words back. Instead I went to the bedroom I shared with Amelia and slammed the door. I sat on the bottom bunk—Amelia's bunk—and stomped my heels on the floor.

Why couldn't Dad get a different job? Nothing could be harder than teaching kids about the boring olden days. If he could teach history, couldn't he sell cars? Or be a sheriff? Or be a *summer* sheriff with Sheriff Duncan so we could still live in

Hayward every summer? That would be perfect! My parents constantly complained about teachers not making enough money. Now Dad couldn't teach. Why didn't he just get a job that paid more money?

Dad didn't care about the cabin. Amelia didn't care. Mom cared but not enough to do something. It was wrong to be ten and the only one who cared.

Then I heard *the word*.

I heard it float from the kitchen right through the bedroom door.

I got off the bunk and pressed my ear against the door. Amelia said it again. "I told you. She's so immature."

Matt said, "Well, she's only like nine or whatever, right?"

Amelia said, "She's almost eleven! See? Christa's so immature people think she's two years younger than she actually is."

Nine? I hated Amelia always telling me to grow up, but this was worse! I took a breath and prepared to show them how mature I could be. You don't have to paint your nails or wear mascara to be mature. I pushed the door open and marched back into the kitchen and smiled all big.

"I was just making sure our bedroom is picked up, and it is. Now I'm back to eat some of Matt's delicious popcorn."

Amelia looked at Matt Cat-Hat and shrugged. Dad patted the seat next to him at the table. "Glad you could join us, sweetie."

While Matt popped the kernels, Amelia melted butter and Mom set out bowls. I picked up the Monopoly pieces and put them in the box. I did it without being asked *and* without saying Amelia should do it since we'd played Monopoly because Matt couldn't do anything else.

But I wasn't done demonstrating my maturity. When everybody was seated at the table with popcorn, I said, quite delightfully, "So, Matt, tell us about yourself."

My parents laughed. Amelia gave me one of her knock-it-off looks, but this was the kind of mature question adults asked all the time. Matt

Chatty-Chat-Chat didn't mind, either. He was one of those young people who liked talking to adults.

"I play hockey on varsity. I need a hockey scholarship because that's the only way I'll ever have money for college."

"What kind of career are you planning?" Mom asked.

Matt's eyes seemed extra big and extra blue as he answered, "I'd like to be a teacher."

My parents smiled as though an angel had opened her wings. Dad said, "It must be hard having a job during hockey season."

"Yeah, but it just got easier. Sally and Neil are way better than old Ed Clark. A guy with a fortune hiding under his mattress should be happier, don't you think?"

"Rumors are very—" Mom started to talk, but I couldn't believe Matt had the story so wrong. I interrupted. "Hiding money under his mattress? Hah! More like money hiding in a wall!" Then I remembered Grumpa had told us to keep it quiet— the hole in the wall, the hundred dollar bills I'd found, the secret fortune. The last thing I needed was Matt Flat-Bat searching for loot. I tried to unsay it. "That was a joke. Money in a wall! Um . . . Knock knock?"

Matt looked confused, but he played along. "Who's there?"

"Money in a wall."

"Money in a wall who?" My brain felt mushy. Matt repeated, "Money in a wall who?" I needed time, so I shoved a fistful of popcorn in my mouth. It's not mature to talk with a mouth full of popcorn. I chewed and chewed and chewed. Matt repeated, "Money in a wall who?"

I swallowed. "I forgot."

"You forgot your own joke?" Amelia rolled her eyes. "Christa, you're too weird."

Dad adjusted his glasses on his nose. Even with the whiskers he looked like a history teacher. "The Clarks are interesting folks. I'd want to get a look around that restaurant. With all the old artifacts upstairs—the Prohibition posters, the china—I'd love to see what's in the basement."

"What's Prohibition?" I asked.

"That's when it was illegal to make and sell alcohol. That law was passed because people used to drink a lot more than they do now. Alcohol caused a lot of problems," Dad said.

"Hah! I guess alcohol made them forget how awful it was to live without television." Everyone laughed at my joke.

"The basement is pretty cool," Matt said. "We're not supposed to go down there, but everybody checks it out eventually. I mean, you have to, right?"

"I would never encourage rule breaking." Dad huddled closer to Matt and grinned like a teenager. "But if the rule's already broken, then you might as well tell me what's down there."

Everyone laughed, even Amelia The Princess, who hadn't laughed at the cabin in two years. I huddled close, too, in case Matt's report revealed big clues.

"The Clarks could open a museum, no joke. The basement is packed. Lots of kitchen things. They've got an old walk-in freezer against the wall that they don't use anymore. It's locked, so you can't get inside. There's a bunch of weird stuff, too. My buddy and I found this old cane. You screw off the top and inside is a glass tube, which people would fill with booze so they could drink it secretly."

"A whiskey cane!" Dad nearly bounced off his chair. "A real whiskey cane? Amazing! What else?"

"Wait a minute," Amelia said. "I thought the Clarks didn't drink when it was illegal to drink. Look at all the old posters on the walls. They still don't sell beer."

"Ed Clark's mother was the anti-booze person," Matt said. "She was part of some church group that started Prohibition and got laws making booze illegal. She was upset when the laws changed back. Cranky Ed sees things her way. But everyone around here knows Ed Clark's father and grandfather were bootleggers. They worked for Al Capone."

I squealed, "And Al Capone built a big house here and even owned an entire lake!"

"I'm surprised you remember that, Christa,"

Mom said. "You were only four when we toured Capone's hideout. It's been closed for years now."

"Alex told me about the house. Or the hideout, whatever you call it. Mr. Edmund Clark has been there. Maybe he was there for a tour, or maybe he was there a long time ago, when the house was used for bootlegging."

"Ed is old, but he's not old enough to have been bootlegging in Capone's hideaway," Dad said. "I'm sure he toured it."

"I don't remember touring it," I said. "I don't remember anything about it."

"How could you forget? I can't." Amelia turned to Matt. "Christa climbed on the sofa and knocked over a lamp. The tour guide asked us to leave."

Dad waved his hand, shooing away any talk that wasn't about artifacts. "So what else is in the basement?"

"Junk, really. Aprons. Pictures. Old menus. Empty kegs. Most snoopers don't care about artifacts or whatever historians call them. They're looking for money, but nobody ever finds anything down there. Everyone in town knows Capone hid money and everyone knows it's scattered all over the place and everyone knows the Clarks took some. It's just not in that basement."

"Interesting." Amelia The Princess yawned because the conversation, I guessed, did not have the excitement of tanning.

"Nan said there's no secret money. I asked her when Alex and I were in the bait shop."

Dad was so interested in Matt's report that he ignored me. "Are there journals? That's where you experience history, you know, reading about people's day-to-day lives." Dad had to be deaf. Matt was talking about money. Who cared about journals and aprons and pictures?

"Journals? Probably," Matt said.

Mom started stacking the empty popcorn bowls. "This is silly. Al Capone killed people for money. I don't think he willy-nilly scattered his fortune around the Northwoods. If he hid money anywhere, it'd be in a safe."

I said it again. "Nan told me there's no secret money at Clarks Pizza."

"Then why are so many people looking for it?" I didn't have an answer to Matt's question. He said, "Personally, I think it's in the tunnels."

My legs practically grew springs. I hollered, "Tunnels? What tunnels?"

"Bootleggers dug tunnels to run booze around," Matt said. "True fact. Nobody's found them, but they're here. Everyone knows it."

Dad shook his head. "That's one of those old legends, Matt. Bootleggers used cars and boats to move their alcohol. They bribed cops, and they had guns. They had secret doors between buildings and some tunnels in the city, but not in the woods. Tunnels would've been too much work. Even if they had dug tunnels, they would've caved in years ago. Bootleggers weren't exactly master engineers."

I slipped out of the conversation because I couldn't stop thinking.

Secret money.

Hideouts.

Basements.

Tunnels.

I looked at Matt, wondering what else he knew. Then Matt looked at me, like he was wondering what else I knew. While my parents cleaned up, Matt and I stared at each other. I didn't trust him, and his eyes said he didn't trust me, either.

THE ATV AND THE ARGUMENT

Alex Clark was the luckiest kid in the world and the entire universe, probably. First he got to live in Hayward, and second his family knew gangsters, and third his grandpa went to a yard sale and bought a used ATV.

"ATV" means all-terrain vehicle. An ATV is like a supersized tricycle only with an engine. It's fast. Tornado fast. You need gas, a helmet, and parental authority to ride it. All I'd wanted was to ask Grumpa about the loot, but then he brought the ATV out of the shed. After that I couldn't think of anything except racing that ATV through the ditches.

All afternoon Grumpa taught Alex how to drive the ATV. And he taught me how to sit behind Alex and not pester him about driving it, too.

"Can we take it on gravel roads?" I asked.

"Maybe."

"Do we have to wear helmets?" The helmet trapped sweat in my hair and made my head itch. "It's so hot."

"Hell's bells, Minnow. I'm surprised your parents don't make you wear a helmet in the shower."

Grumpa, Alex, and I left the ATV by the shed and walked to the porch for something to drink. Wisconsin summers drenched everything with a warm mist. Humidity. The air was sweating, basically. Grumpa drank water, but Alex and I downed cold orange sodas.

Alex let out a refreshing orange-soda burp and said, "Now that I know how to drive an ATV, can I drive the speedboat?"

"One thing at a time."

"Grumpa, why can't I drive the ATV and have Alex ride behind me?"

Grumpa took off his fishing hat and wiped the sweat from his forehead. He didn't have much hair. Why didn't he let the wind blow the little strands around? "Minnow, you have an unmagic touch. I don't need you driving an ATV through my shed."

"I won't! I'll be careful. Very, very careful."

"Let's review history. Four summers ago, you put a baseball through my kitchen window. Three summers ago, you tried to set the lawn on fire with a magnifying glass. Two summers ago, you—"

"None of those accidents involved an all-terrain vehicle!"

Alex dropped to the grass and rolled around laughing. He had a stupid laugh. He hee-haw laughed like a sick mule. "Set the grass on fire? Oh my God! Hilarious!"

"Okay, kids, enough. I've got fish on ice in the shed. They ain't going to clean themselves," Grumpa said. "Go find something to do."

CHASING AL CAPONE'S GANG THROUGH
THE STREETS OF CHICAGO

The Adventure: Motorcycle police trying to arrest Capone and his crooks

The Place: The busiest street in Chicago (Grumpa's driveway)

The Characters: Chase Truegood (me) and Buck Punch (Alex)

The Wardrobe/Props: Motorcycle (the not-moving, not-running ATV), police badges (pickle jar covers with duct tape), handcuffs (Amelia's headbands), police guns (squirt guns), helmets (helmets), and rope (rope)

Chase Truegood and Buck Punch have survived many adventures, but trying to arrest Al Capone and his gang might be their last.

Sheriff Duncan assigned the team to the Capone case. Capone escaped the long arm of the law whenever Sheriff Duncan tried to arrest him. It was up to Chase and Buck to get Capone once and for all.

Chase and Buck parked their motorcycle outside a bar where Capone was selling his illegal booze.

"This stakeout might be our most dangerous," Buck said. "I think Capone knows we're undercover."

"Me, too. But Sheriff Duncan will fire us if we don't stay on the case. I can't afford to lose this job. I'd have to sell the orphanage, and all the kids would be homeless."

"Chase! Look! It's Capone leaving the bar."

"And his assistants, too!"

Capone strutted down the sidewalk with his assistants Matt Fat-Cat and Mr. Walt Miller. Capone got in the backseat of his limousine while Mr. Walt Miller loaded cases of booze in the trunk. The driver rolled down the window, and that driver was Chase's sister Jade.

"Jade lied." Chase pointed at the limo. "She didn't leave us to explore the Amazon. She's actually working for Capone!"

"I knew it!" Buck said.

"I knew it first!" Chase said.

"I learned how to detect liars back in Arizona,"

Buck shouted. "But I don't have time to explain it to you. They're driving away. We have to go!"

The team raced down a busy Chicago street in hot pursuit of Capone. Their motorcycle weaved in and out of traffic, barely missing a semitruck carrying dynamite. Buck steered onto the sidewalk to avoid hitting a school bus.

"Time to let me drive," Chase shouted. "We might have to jump a ramp. That's my special skill."

"We'll lose sight of Capone if I stop. We gotta keep moving!"

"Look!" Chase pointed. "Capone is stopping for gas. Pull over!"

"I'll circle the gas station."

"No!" Chase shouted. "I have to drive. Only I understand where Jade might drive the limo. We must change places!"

Buck got off the motorcycle and switched spots with Chase. She straddled the bike and clenched the handlebars. Then off they zoomed! Soon they were inches from Capone's bumper. Buck pulled out his gun and fired, trying to hit the tires of the limo.

"You hit a bump!" Buck shrieked as he fell off the cycle and rolled in the dirt.

The motorcycle tipped as Chase slammed the brakes. It slid on its side, nearly taking off Chase's head as it skidded under a semi. She leaped off the cycle and emerged unhurt on the other side of the truck.

"Buck?" Chase dropped to her knees to check on her partner.

He sputtered and coughed. "I knew you were a bad driver . . . but . . . didn't wanna say . . . didn't wanna make you mad."

"What's going on?"

Standing a few feet away was Neil, his face screwed into the maddest of mad expressions. We hadn't noticed our parents' cars pulling into the driveway.

"Nothing." Alex stood up and brushed the dirt off his shorts. Neil just stared until Alex said, "Dad, it's just an ATV."

"I know what it is. Where in the world did it come from?"

"Grandpa," Alex said. "Grandpa gave it to me."

While Neil yelled, and Grumpa yelled back, Mom took me by the hand and led me into the cabin for dinner.

Neil shouted that there's no way Alex would be allowed to drive that thing, even if he's slow and careful, because he could get killed. Then Grumpa said parents should stop treating kids like fine china and let them have some fun. Then Neil said kids' safety is more important than fun. Then Grumpa said if Alex hadn't been living in Aristona all this time he could've been spoiling the kid a long time ago. Then Neil yelled at Grumpa about being forced to work when he was a kid and never having a real childhood. Then Grumpa said they'd fished together sometimes on Sundays and wasn't that fun, dammit?

Mom shut the windows, and I couldn't hear the rest.

THE LOOT AND THE SECRET

We had Grumpa cornered, basically. He was watching TV in his recliner, away from the distraction of broken pipes and the canoe rescue and the ATV. So we pounced.

"Tell us about the loot! Pleeeeeeease! Tell us!" Alex begged.

"Go find something to do. I want my nap."

Grumpa slept every afternoon in the recliner. He napped with his gray fishing hat on his head, his hands folded on his chest, and the remote control on his lap. Before his nap, he had a cheese sandwich, potato chips, and an orange soda. He ate on paper towels so he didn't make dirty dishes. Every day, it was the same lunch, served on paper towels, followed by a nap. I liked this about Grumpa. He didn't need to change things all the time.

"Go on. Out." Grumpa waved his arm at us.

Alex looked at me and shrugged. I couldn't believe he was going to give up so easily. I cleared my throat and said, "Why'd your mom use the words 'blood money'?"

"Hell's bells. The past is the past."

"But it's history!" I said. "History is important."

"Family history's real important," Alex added. "I lived in Arizona too long. Nobody told me about the money. Does Dad know?"

Grumpa turned down the volume on the TV. "History my rear end. You kids can't resist a secret, and these days you don't have to. You just type on that Internet, and the computer tells you everything whether it ought to or not. You ever heard of skeletons in the closet?"

We shook our heads.

"We used to call family secrets 'skeletons in the closet,' and we kept our mouths shut and the skeletons stayed put. I sure as heck didn't tell your dad, Alex. We were busy earning a living, and I didn't need my boy running around town looking for trouble."

"Okay. Just wondering," Alex said. He turned and walked past the recliner. I grabbed his arm before he could leave the room.

"I think Alex is saying he doesn't know anything about his family. He's counting on you to tell him."

"I'm just wondering is all," Alex said. "Just wondering."

Grumpa sighed all big. Finally he turned off the television, and we sat on the old shag carpet, ready for the story. He pointed at a picture on the wall behind the sofa. It was an old wedding photo, from the time when pictures were black and white and people wore funny hats. The people weren't smiling, and their eyes looked hard, so I knew right away they had to be Grumpa's parents.

"Those are my parents, Ernie and Hillary. You heard the phrase about a person working hard as a horse? Well, my mother worked harder than a hundred horses. She was like my wife, Ginny. They both believed honest work made a good life. They were kind and smart and good to the core. My mother always said, 'What good is it for a man to gain the whole world, yet forfeit his soul'?"

"That sounds like Dr. Phil," Alex said. "Mom watches him on TV."

"It's from the Bible!" Grumpa grumped. "Don't they teach you anything at school? It means money ain't everything."

Grumpa put the recliner's footrest down and dropped his feet to the floor. Alex looked at me and cleared his throat. I reached into my back pocket and pulled out a piece of history—a wrapped candy anise ball.

I had a few of those disgusting balls in the back of a drawer. Last year at the candy store, Dad had told me anise balls were popular in the olden days, so I decided to try a few. And what I learned was kids in the olden days did not have taste buds, because anise balls tasted like cough syrup.

I held the anise ball in front of Grumpa's face. Not a bribe, Alex had said, but a gift from two nice kids. Kids who cared.

"Now what in the world is that?"

"We got it for you, Grumpa. An anise ball. Candy from the olden days." I held it under his nose, the way you tease a dog with a meatball you don't want to eat because Mom cooked it in mushroom gravy.

Sure enough, Grumpa reached out his hand and took the candy. He peeled off the wrapper and popped it in his mouth. Either he smiled a little or the anise ball forced his mouth muscles to move. His eyes seemed to soften and lose focus. I wondered if the anise balls were bringing him back to the olden days. Then he said, "What I'm about to tell you kids has never been spoken. I guess it don't matter much anymore. Everyone who knew anything is dead."

AL CAPONE AND THE CLARK FAMILY LOOT

Years ago, people drank a lot of alcohol. They drank like stray cats in front of bowls of milk. Some of them drank so much they became mean and stupid. Those drunks weren't taking care of their families. My mother, Hillary Clark, believed if drinking was against the law, then people wouldn't do it. Lots of people saw it her way. So the government banned alcohol, but the whole plan backfired.

Nobody likes to be told what to do. When you can't have something, you want it even more. And if people want something and they got money to buy it, someone will find a way to make and sell it. Don't matter what the law says. So people kept drinking. Since they couldn't buy alcohol in stores or bars, they bought it from crooks.

Let me tell you, it was a good time for crooks. There was a fortune to be made selling booze. They called it bootlegging. Al Capone was king of the bootleggers. He was tough and mean, and he'd do anything to earn a buck. Capone didn't work alone, of course. He needed helpers. He needed guns and fists and booze and secret bars and ways to deliver booze to those secret bars.

In the Northwoods, two of his helpers were my father and grandfather.

My family ran a nice restaurant in the same spot as Clarks Pizza. You would have needed to go to Duluth to find anything nicer. We served sirloin steaks—never fillets—because sirloins have the most flavor. Pops cooked them in bacon grease. Capone said our sirloins were better than any restaurant's in Chicago.

We never quit selling booze, even when it was illegal. We moved the bar into the basement. My mother thought alcohol ruined lives, but Pops loved it. He couldn't get enough. He liked drinking it even more than he liked selling it.

If you wanted in to our secret bar, you had to knock on the basement door and say the code words. If you said, *"Is this the bathroom?"* the door would open, and you could go drink booze downstairs. If you didn't know the code, the door wouldn't open.

Every time that door opened, Capone and my family made money. I don't know how much we raked in, but Capone had so much money here and in Chicago he could barely count it. Capone didn't want the government to know how much money he had, so he didn't use banks or accountants. He stashed it away. Capone was so tough, nobody was stupid enough to steal from him. The man was a killer.

Eventually Capone went crazy from a disease in his brain. He started seeing ghosts and yelling and acting like a lunatic. Ghosts weren't the only things after him. The cops were on his tail. Crazy Al knew he'd get busted. He worried constantly about his money. So he started hiding it. Some here, some there. He hid it in safes and walls. Hell, he even buried some of it! He gave it to his buddies to hide for him, but he expected them to hold on to it and give it back.

He gave some of his money to Pops.

Hell's bells, that's enough because who even cares anymore. Some things are best left alone, and all the talk about Capone and the Clarks is history and it's nuts to bring it up again.

That's how Grumpa stopped the story.

He picked up the remote and turned on his programs. With a wave of his hand, he told us to go outside. But we weren't ready to give up. He hadn't told us everything.

Alex said, "So all these people with Capone's money figured he'd never have a chance to claim it, right?"

"Finders keepers," I said.

"Except the finders were all crooks, too," Alex said. "Grandpa, will you please finish the story?"

Grumpa leaned toward us. "So you want to hear more?"

We nodded all eager.

"Alrighty. Come closer." We wiggled toward his feet. "Little closer. That's good." He bent his head down. "BOO!"

I shrieked, and Alex fell backward. Grumpa laughed so hard he coughed and thumped his chest.

We drank orange sodas in the kitchen, waiting for Grumpa to take his nap. When the snoring started, it was time for our plan. Grumpa had banned us from the basement after the pipes exploded, but we needed to conduct a full search. If Grumpa's mother left traces of money in the basement, then maybe she left clues, too.

Quietly we went downstairs. The basement smelled damp from the water-pipe explosion. A section of new pipes had been put in the ceiling, but the washtub hadn't been replaced. The tub was propped up on cement blocks to cover the hole. I walked to Grumpa's workbench where a new taxidermy project was underway. A raccoon had been nearly stuffed, but its eyes hadn't been glued in place. The thing stood on its back legs with its paws in the air.

Alex grabbed my arm as I reached out to touch it. "Stop! We'll get in trouble."

"How's he going to know that I touched it? I just want to touch it, that's all. Not move it."

"He'll know. He's got a nose for that. Just look

for clues, okay? I'll start in the room where he turned off the water."

Alex went around the stairs. Before I could move, he poked his head around the corner and said, "His mother taught him taxidermy and gave him his first tools. That's why he makes a big deal out of it. Don't touch his stuff."

"His *mother* knew taxidermy?"

"Don't touch his stuff."

"I heard you the first time."

I so wanted to touch his stuff. He'd spread it all over the long table. Glue. Fake animal eyes. Gloves. Knives. Pins. Screws. Wood boards. Bottles and bottles of stuff like "flocking adhesive," whatever that was. It just sat there, all alone, begging for someone to touch it.

But I didn't because I found something almost as good: boxes along the wall labeled *taxidermy*. Or, like Dad would say, *artifacts*.

Most of the boxes contained supplies like the ones on the table. One box wasn't cardboard, though. It was an old-fashioned wood trunk. Inside were taxidermy supplies—old taxidermy supplies. I could tell they were old because the metal tools were rusted, and the bottles were glass instead of plastic. Carefully I peeled back the cloth wrapped around objects in the box. They were small taxidermied birds, chipmunks, and squirrels. Each one was mounted on a wood board etched with the words *For My Edmund.* They must have been gifts from Mrs. Hillary Clark to Grumpa.

For almost an hour, Alex and I dug through boxes. He found a few *For My Edmund* animals, too, and one notebook. "I can hardly read what's in here," he said, holding up the notebook. "Everything's in tiny cursive."

"What's it say?"

"Just a bunch of dumb recipes and prayers and stuff about weather."

The ceiling creaked. Footsteps. Grumpa's footsteps.

"I think Grumpa's awake!"

Alex whispered, "Put everything back."

We made quick work of straightening boxes while he walked back and forth.

"How are we going to get upstairs without him seeing us?" I asked.

Alex shrugged.

"Stop shrugging and start coming up with ideas for a change! I can't always be the idea person."

"Actually, I'm the idea person," Alex said. "You just talk faster."

Alex always tried to show me up. It was annoying. I said, "Here's an idea. We're going to tiptoe up the steps. Then we'll be ready to get out of here when he's in the bathroom or something."

Ever so slowly we walked up the steps, which creaked but probably not loud enough for old ears to notice. I leaned against the door and listened for clues that Grumpa might be in the kitchen—water running, refrigerator opening and closing, micro-wave beeping. Nothing.

I whispered, "It's quiet, Alex. I think it's safe."

I nudged the door open.

There he was. Grumpa. Arms crossed, staring at the door, waiting. Alex gasped.

"Out!" Grumpa pointed to the kitchen. We got out fast. Airplane fast. We stood next to the stove and looked very, very sorry. "Did you touch my taxidermy?"

"No," I said.

"No," Alex said.

"I told you to stay out of the basement. Do your ears need cleaning?"

"No," I said.

"No," Alex said.

"Around here we have consequences for not listening."

Alex and I looked at each other. After we broke the pipes and sunk the canoe and trespassed in the basement, Grumpa might have something terrible in mind. Neil had told Alex that Grumpa had no patience. Grumpa's face squished together like he was thinking hard. He looked at Alex and then me and then Alex and then me. He waved his finger at us and said, "You break one more rule and you'll find out what those consequences are."

I bit my lip to stop myself from smiling.

There were no consequences.

Grumpa was a real grandparent, clearly.

Grumpa sent us outside with a stack of cookies and more orange soda. I sat on the porch steps and drank from my can while Alex took off his shoes and socks. He tromped around in a circle on the grass.

He said, "The only good thing about living here is you can walk around outside and not worry about stepping on scorpions or tarantulas. In Arizona you either wear shoes or you die. There's nothing scary here."

I was tired of hearing Alex talk about Arizona. Nothing scary in the Northwoods? Obviously he'd never read a book about Wisconsin. "Around here we don't need shoes, but we have tornadoes that will suck you into outer space."

"We had tornadoes, too. Dust tornadoes. Those

are worse because they will suck you into outer space, and your eyes will be scratched by dust."

"When it rains in Wisconsin sometimes it rains so hard and so fast that it washes away entire towns. Who knows? There could be a town under Whitefish Lake from the olden days."

"In Arizona—"

"It doesn't rain in Arizona, Alex."

"There are black widow spiders in Arizona!"

"Stop it!" I shouted. "If you like Arizona more then you should just move back! You get to live here, and you're too stupid to care."

My head felt full of flames. If Alex had flames in his head, he didn't act like it. He bent down and picked up a rock. He calmly said, "Maybe I will move back. When you leave I won't know anyone and I'll probably never know anyone. I'll just run away and live in Arizona so I'll have something to do."

"Good. Then you can hang around with . . ." I couldn't remember the names of Alex's friends.

"You can be with those guys! What are their stupid names?"

Alex looked blank.

"Their names? What are your friends' names?"

"Um . . . Billy. My friend is Billy."

"Billy and who else?"

He threw the rock across the lawn, across the gravel driveway, toward Olivia Stanger's sign. He missed, and the rock landed on the edge of the grass by our driveway. He threw another rock and missed with that one, too. Finally he said, "Nobody else. It's just me and Billy. We don't play with other kids much. They're annoying and weird."

I knew what Alex was really saying: The other kids didn't play with Alex and Billy. The other kids called *them* annoying and weird. I knew this because it's what happened to me at my school. The girls in my class traded bracelets made from rubber bands, and somehow I was the weird one. Playtime at school was messed up. The cabin was simple.

"Oh," I said. "I know what that's like. Annoying and weird kids, I mean."

"Who cares? I don't."

"Me, either."

I was glad Alex understood, but it also felt like one of those awkward moments. We'd admitted we were too weird to have lots of friends, basically. Who wants to admit that? So I changed the subject. "Alex, why won't Grumpa tell us the whole story? What happened after his father got the loot? How'd it end up in a wall?"

"He just doesn't talk much. Dad says he's been like that since my grandma died."

"I don't understand why he wouldn't just finish the story. What's a few more words?"

"He must be extra tired. I can tell. He forgot a bunch of stuff today, like we were supposed to have carrots with our sandwiches. And he forgot we're supposed to stay inside and watch a movie this afternoon."

"That's stupid. Why would we stay inside? We never stay inside unless it's storming."

Alex's eyes got all big. I knew that big-eyed look. It's the look people get when they almost blow a secret.

"What? Why are we supposed to stay inside, Alex?"

Alex picked up another rock and threw it harder. Still, he missed Olivia Stanger's sign. "Pretend I didn't tell you, but people are coming to look at your cabin later today."

I froze. My parents were keeping a secret from me, the most important secret of my life. The cabin sale was happening so fast. Grumpa hadn't even finished the whole Capone story. I needed that story. If there was gangster money hidden in Hayward and the gangsters were dead, then it was finders keepers. There might be enough money to pay my parents' bills and keep the cabin—maybe enough to do all that *and* buy Nan's Bait and Tackle. But the important thing was saving the cabin.

"When are they coming? Are you sure?"

"Even Grandpa doesn't want people looking at your cabin," Alex said. "He thinks you're a pain, but he says new people will be worse. They'll probably be from a big city and so stupid they'll need expensive fishing radars to catch anything."

I blinked away the eye sweats. "I hate that kids don't get to make any decisions. My parents decided all by themselves to sell the cabin. Didn't even ask what I thought. They aren't even sorry."

"Parents are never sorry. They never apologize for nothing. They think they're right about everything. My parents didn't even ask if I wanted to move. They just announced it one day like it was the best thing in the world."

"At least you got to move here," I said. "And you get to have babysitting by a grandpa instead of a stupid summer program."

"Well, he's an old grandpa and sometimes a scary one."

"He gave you an ATV."

"Yeah, and my dad took it away. Dad's being the mean one. Grandpa's not half as bad as he says."

I stared at the cabin and wondered about Capone's fortune. Al Capone could have enough money hiding in northern Wisconsin to save hundreds of cabins, and Grumpa might be the only person still alive with information. I needed more time.

"Aren't you going to do something?" Alex asked.

I felt tired, so tired I could probably only run three miles. That was not like me at all.

Alex poked me. "Well?"

"I'm thinking! Here's your chance to be the idea person, Alex."

He thought for a few minutes, then grinned. "What if they don't *want* to buy it? What if they don't like what they see?"

I was going to ask what he meant, but his grin turned into a wicked smile. If I read his mind correctly, Alex was the coolest friend in the world, pretty much.

THE FIASCO AND EAVESDROPPING

We did the job fast. No talking, no goofing. No time for Chase Truegood or Buck Punch. Then we hid behind Grumpa's shed and waited for the cabin shoppers.

There's nothing to do when you're hiding behind a shed. We caught bugs and put them in a big glass jar so we could see which bugs would eat the others. Believe it or not, the ladybug is the meanest bug. Ladybugs devour other bugs and then buzz around all classy.

Olivia Stanger was a ladybug.

Finally we heard car wheels on gravel, doors opening and closing, and voices. Happy voices. Alex and I peeked around the shed and saw Olivia Stanger with a man and a woman wearing neat city clothes, just like Grumpa predicted. The woman had high-heeled shoes, and the guy's hair was slicked up and tossed around like a model's.

The lady was already texting. I could imagine it: *We're here! Outside looks nice! Hope it has a toilet LOL.*

I crossed my arms. Soon she would not be LOLing.

Minutes later, they skedaddled out of the cabin with frowns on their faces.

Alex and I rolled on the grass laughing. It wasn't funny for very long, though. An hour later, when my parents drove up to the cabin, even the car looked angry.

"Christa Boyd-Adams!" Dad yelled. "What were you thinking?"

I was thinking, *Hooray! Alex and I are geniuses!* But that's not what my face and body showed. I stood with droopy shoulders in the kitchen, wearing my extra-extra-extra sorry face, while my parents took turns yelling at me.

"Worms in the sinks?" Dad waved his arms around. "That's beyond disgusting."

Mom looked at me like she didn't know who I was. "And fish guts? In a glass bowl? On the table? Do you have any idea how long it'll take to air the stink out of the cabin? It's . . . it's . . ." She looked at Dad. "I can't even finish that sentence."

"Where did you get the taxidermied animals? The ballet-dancing squirrel made the woman scream. Yes, she screamed."

Then it was Mom's turn. "And you'll be thrilled to hear Olivia Stanger fired us! She was particularly offended that her teeth were blacked out on her sign. I've never even heard of a realtor dropping a property—ever. That's how awful this is. I supposed you're pleased with yourself."

I needed the eye sweats to help me out of this mess. My dad always went soft when I looked sad. I pinched my leg as hard as I could.

"Don't even think this changes anything,

Christa Boyd-Adams," she said. "We've already called a new realtor, and he's coming tomorrow. What do you have to say for yourself?"

I hadn't prepared for a new realtor thief. Alex and I had been out-geniused. I gulped. "Well, I didn't know the fish guts would take forever to air out of the cabin, and it sure does stink in here. That's bad. I'm sorry. Very sorry."

Dad paced the small kitchen, around and around the table. He turned on the fan and set it to blow out the window, taking some of the fish stink with it. "Your mother and I want you to write a letter of apology to Olivia. It won't change anything, but you're going to do it anyway."

But there was a problem. A big problem. My parents had seen the worms in the sinks, the zanimals on the furniture, and the fish-gut centerpiece on the table, but they didn't say anything—not a word—about the snake Alex put in the bathtub. He'd snatched up that snake without blinking. If the snake was no longer in the bathtub, I had a snake escape on my hands. Snakes are the most terrifying things on the planet, which is why I didn't like them.

Dad continued, "Under normal circumstances, I'd be tempted to ground you for a month, but . . . but it's our last summer here, and I can't stand the thought of your being locked up inside."

Still not a word about the snake. Was it a trick? Were they holding back to see if I'd confess?

"Did you hear me, Christa?"

"What?"

"I'm tempted to ground you for a month."

How long would he be tempted to ground me if a snake slithered across the kitchen? Two months? Three months?

Mom snapped her fingers to get my attention. "Christa? Your father is talking to you."

"I'm listening. I just feel too bad to talk."

"Did Alex help you with this fiasco?" Mom asked.

The worst ending to this fiasco would be me ratting out Alex to my parents, especially about the snake escape. My parents would rat out Alex to his parents. His parents might ground him for a month, because it wasn't *his* last summer here, and what would I do all summer by myself?

"No. I didn't have a helper in this fiasco."

I was basically telling the truth. This fiasco had been Alex's idea, which made him the idea person for a change and me the helper for a change. Mom never asked the right questions.

My parents sent me to bed early. I threw a fit, not a full-blown fit, just a little fit, so they'd think they'd been really tough on me. But I was happy not to be grounded for a month. I also was happy to have the top bunk. A snake couldn't climb up the metal pole and slither into bed with me, but maybe it could get into the bottom bunk. Amelia's bunk. If she saw a snake, her glittery nails might curl up and catch fire. She'd freak out and scream and cry and text all her stupid friends.

Better her than me.

I was afraid of snakes, especially nighttime snakes. When you're sleeping, and it's dark, and you feel something tickling your arm, and it's a snake, well, that's just too much. That's a moment for screaming, even if you're me. I was fearless except for snakes and sharks, which is why I will always be a lake person and never an ocean person.

It was too early to sleep, so I got up and pressed my ear against the door. I figured Mom and Dad would be talking about me.

For at least fifteen minutes, all my parents talked about was Amelia The Princess going out with Matt Drat-Fat. Then they talked about some students. Finally—finally!—they talked about me and the cabin.

Mom said, "It's hard to be angry with her. I get it. I don't want to sell the cabin, either. It breaks my heart."

Dad was all quiet. There was a long, long pause. I made a tiny crack in the door because I couldn't hear. If I shut one eye, I could see just a sliver of the kitchen where they stood talking.

Mom hugged Dad. After about a minute of that, she pulled away and put her hands on his face and said, "It'll be okay, honey. It will."

My dad was crying. *Crying!* I almost gasped. I'd never seen him cry. Ever, and I mean ever.

"It's my fault," he said, wiping his face with the palm of his hand. "I'm sorry I've let you down, all of you. Guess nobody wants to hire a history teacher."

"Sweetheart, please. Don't do this. It's not your fault."

"I should've gone into Dad's construction business. The old man was right. Following your passion won't pay the bills."

"You would've been miserable. You wouldn't be the man I love. The man we love." She kept talking, but my ears buzzed. I didn't want to hear more. I backed up and sat on Amelia's bunk.

I'd thought if they'd wanted to save the cabin, they could. I didn't think they wanted to save the cabin and actually *couldn't*. I felt a new kind of scary, and this scary wasn't like nighttime snakes or sharks.

THE NEW REALTOR THIEF AND YONDER GOLD

I glared at Shawn Weller's picture on the for-sale sign. His blue eyes sparkled, and his big smile showed teeth straight as fence posts. Bright-white fence posts.

"I hope you don't have a problem with my sign."

The voice was Shawn Weller himself. I dropped the stick I was holding. I'd thought he was in the cabin talking to my parents.

"I don't have a problem with your sign," I said. "I like it. Your sign is big. It gives you the face of a giant."

"That's so people can see it from the road."

"Very smart," I said.

Even though I was sweating through my tank top, Shawn Weller wore a brown suit with a tie. His face shined from the heat. I was never, ever going to be a realtor because I didn't want to steal or sweat that much.

He picked up the stick I'd dropped. "When I was a kid, we'd find sticks like this and some rocks and use them to play baseball."

"The game is easier with a bat and ball."

"Agreed." Shawn Weller took a handkerchief from his pocket and wiped his forehead. "I hear you're not very happy about selling this cabin. I understand. It's a great place. I wouldn't want to sell it, either."

I was suspicious. This was the stuff adults said when they were about to trick you into liking them or doing something you didn't want to do.

"Then maybe you should buy it and donate it to us."

He laughed. "I wish I could do that. I would if I could. Your name is Kristin, right?"

"Yeah. Kristin Kristine Kristopher Boyd-Adams."

"It is not!"

That voice was my mother. My sighing, head-shaking mother. I hadn't heard her come outside.

"I apologize for my daughter's manners, Shawn," Mom said. "I promise you'll have no problems from her whatsoever. Am I right, Christa?"

Before I could agree and promise and all that, there came a man-scream from the cabin: "ARRRRGH!"

The door opened, and Dad leaped outside, gasping. Mom rushed to him. "Todd! What's wrong?"

A little shiver went through his body. "I think my imagination got the best of me. I thought I saw a snake." A little shiver went through my body, too.

Mom said, "A snake? Are you certain?"

"Never mind. That's crazy. It was just a shadow, I'm sure. Guess I need new glasses."

Shawn Weller looked concerned. "Are there any cracks in the foundation that need to be sealed?"

That's when I walked away. It was messed up. My dad crying. Amelia The Princess acting crazy about Matt Hat-Gnat. The snake escape. A new realtor for the cabin. Even Chase Truegood couldn't fix this mess. It seemed like it was all my fault, definitely.

PANNING FOR GOLD IN AL CAPONE'S RIVER

The Adventure: Cowboys seeking a fortune
The Place: The Arizona River in gold country (lakeshore)
The Characters: Chase Truegood (me) and Buck Punch (Alex)
The Wardrobe/Props: Western vests (life jackets), cowboy hats (Mom's sun hats), panning-for-gold pans (pie pans), gold extraction tools (spoons, forks, noodle strainer), guns (sticks), and rope (rope)

Chase Truegood and Buck Punch have survived many adventures, but pannin' for gold in yonder Arizona, in Al Capone's own river, may be their last. Outlaws hid in them thar mountains, along with cowboy-killin' lions.

Buck swept off his hat. "Sun's burnin' me up." Then he spat some chewin' tobacco.

"Can't be givin' up yet," Chase said. "We ain't got no gold."

The old-timer had told 'em the Arizona River was overflowin' with gold, but no cowboys were done brave enough to pan it. Capone and bandit-assistants Mr. Walt Miller and Matt Splat-That scoured the area stealin' and shootin' and drinkin' and killin' and fightin' with each other. Worse, Capone had hypnotized Chase's sister Jade and done made her a bandit, too.

Chase dug her pan in the sand, swirlin' it just so, and dumped the mush into the sand strainer. "Buck, that thar's a piece of gold."

Buck licked the rock. "Old-timers say gold be tastin' like maple syrup. This thar rock tastes like snake soup."

"How long can we be survivin' with no gold? We ain't got no money for supplies and grits."

Buck jumped up and pointed yonder. "Bandits! It be Capone, Chase."

Chase looked yonder, where four bandits peaked over rocks. Known as the best shot in the western territory, Chase whipped her gun and fired yonder. "I got Mr. Walt Miller, and I done wounded Jade! I mighta knocked the hypnosis right out of her head."

Chase looked around. "Buck?"

Buck was floating facedown in the river. Chase pulled his vest with the strength of a passel of horses. "Buck? You done hurt?"

"Capone done got me. Right thar in the heart."

Chase fired more rounds. "I got 'em all. Right thar in the heads."

"Capone done got away," Buck gasped. "I seen him gallopin' on his horse with gold and booze."

"Buck, ya need heart-repair rub. I bought it from the old-timer at yonder camp because I'm your best buddy." Chase pulled off his pannin' vest and smacked her hand against his heart. "Thar! You're done fine now!"

"My . . . leg . . ."

"What be wrong with yer leg? Yer bleedin' from the chest."

"Got bit by a mountain lion lookin' for firewood. Didn't wanna be sayin'." Buck gasped again. He pulled a rock from his pocket. "Been wantin' to surprise ya."

Chase inspected it. "What's this thar rock?"

"Tastes like maple. It's gold!" He moaned. "Enough for ya to git a stagecoach back east."

"A real partner wouldn't be leavin' ya in the Arizona River!"

"If I got to die, Chase, I want to be dyin' right here. Right in yonder Arizona. The old-timer can bury me."

"He don't know where to find ya!"

"Tell 'em . . . tell 'em to follow them thar vultures."

"Don't be dyin' Buck!"

"For the love of Gertrude! Who's Buck and why is he dying?" Grumpa stood on the dock, looking concerned.

"We're just goofing around," Alex said.

"Want to play?" I asked. "You could be Buck's grandfather, Mr. Edmund Punch."

"I'm too old for nonsense. And you got company. That cousin of Matt's is here. His parents just dropped him off. They must think I'm running a daycare."

Alex splashed to shore and dropped his life jacket on the rocks. He didn't even look back. Just ran toward the house.

"Hop out, Minnow. You can't be out here alone."

"I'm wearing a life jacket."

"Are you trying to get me arrested for neglect?"

"Alex is the one who can't swim good. I swim great. Who's Matt's cousin and why's he here?"

"Neil and Sally want Alex to meet some kids before school starts. Matt volunteered his cousin." Grumpa pointed at me, then the dock. "Out."

"Fine." I pulled myself up on the dock and dried my face on a towel.

"Before you come over, go change your clothes. Then you can meet Quincy."

QUINCY AND THE TREE

No, I didn't like him, even his name. Quincy didn't rhyme with anything, except *mincy*, and *mincy* is not a real word, probably. Quincy. It was the name you gave your baby if you wanted that baby to grow up stealing friends and hogging them and ignoring everyone else.

Quincy had cropped brown hair like Alex, but he was short and solid while Alex was tall and skinny. If those boys were reptiles, Alex would be a gecko and Quincy would be a toad.

Right away, Quincy said to Alex, "Are you

grounded all summer? Is that why you have to play with a girl?"

Alex shrugged. We were standing on the porch, just checking each other out. I looked at Quincy's legs because I could tell everything about kids when they wore shorts. Scratches, bruises, bug bites, and dirt on legs were good signs. Extra points for Band-Aids. Quincy's legs were pasty white and unmarked. That meant he was a boring video-game player and inside-loving wimp. He proved me right by saying, "I brought my new game player and my old one just in case."

"Just in case what?" Alex asked.

"In case yours is broke," Quincy said. "We've got two."

Grumpa came from the house carrying a plastic bottle. He handed the bottle to Alex. Sunscreen.

"Your parents say you're supposed to use this goop." He shook his head. "That's my latest crime. Guess you were supposed to be covering yourself in sun lotion every day. Hell's bells. When did the sun become poison?"

Alex squirted some lotion in his hand, smeared it on his arms, and dabbed his cheeks. Quincy grumbled, "I don't want to play outside. It's hot."

"The great outdoors is God's daycare," Grumpa said.

"I probably don't need sunscreen here because the sun in Wisconsin isn't like the sun in Arizona. In Arizona it's so hot—

"I know, I know. The moisture gets sucked right out of your eyeballs," I said.

"Doesn't matter," Grumpa said. "You've got to use this stuff otherwise I'll get fired and I don't want to get fired."

"From what?" I asked.

"From my summer job." Grumpa rubbed lotion into Alex's cheeks where it'd collected in white patches. He squirted a blob on the back of Alex's neck and rubbed that around, too. "I think you're now safe from the horror of the sun. Go find something to do."

Grumpa went back inside and let the door slam

behind him. The three of us looked at each other. I asked, "What should we do?"

Alex shrugged.

Quincy stared at me. "Let's play hide and seek."

"Hide and seek is for babies," I said with a snort.

"Not babies," Alex said. "You can play hide and seek until first grade, I think. Then if you don't stop there's probably something wrong with you."

Quincy snorted back at me. "*Indoor* hide and seek is for babies. Outdoor is more like a treasure hunt."

I nodded because I agreed with this theory, actually.

"Okay, good," Quincy said. "I'll count and you two hide. Whoever is found first has to admit she is a loser."

"Or *he* is a loser." My hands squeezed into fists. "Why do you get to seek? Why don't you hide?"

Quincy thought about it. "Oh, yeah, I get it. Not fair. Um . . . we'll each be the seeker three times and the hider three times. Whoever is found first the most times has to make a sign and write 'I am a loser' on it with her name."

"Or *his* name," I said.

Alex shrugged.

"Excellent!" Quincy shouted and held up his hand for a high five. Alex gave him the wimpiest high five I'd ever seen.

Quincy stood on the porch, covered his eyes, and faced the front door. He started counting. Alex and I sprinted in different directions. Maybe it wasn't fair, but I had an edge. I knew every inch of the Clarks' yard, our yard, Westman Drive, the lakeshore, the woods that surrounded us, and Westman's public boat landing on the other side of the trees. I ran down the slope toward shore. I tip-toed on the dock so Quincy wouldn't hear the metal clanging. I slipped into Grumpa's speedboat and lay on the floor. Quincy would never think to look in the boat.

The boat swayed with the waves rolling toward shore. I wondered how I could make this moment stay with me. When the cabin was gone, I needed memories that felt real. I wanted to be able to close my eyes and see the sky stretched pure and blue. I wanted to hear raindrops plopping fat and lazy on the lake. A camera couldn't make it real. Pictures just teased people. I needed to see and hear and smell and feel.

When I realized I was sleepy, I sat upright so fast I nearly launched myself out of the boat. It'd been too long. Way too long. Where was Quincy? And Alex? I hadn't even heard them looking by the shore. Something was fishy, and it wasn't the lake. I'd fallen for the oldest trick in the book: the hide-and-never-seek. Quincy had sent me away with no plan to find me. And Alex never came looking, either.

Those boys were meaner than a hundred Olivia Stangers. I didn't get out of the boat right away. I had to think and think hard.

Quincy and Alex were sitting on the porch swing with their faces in video game players. I hopped up on the porch steps one at a time and threw my arms in the air. "I won! I won! You couldn't find me!"

"Guess so," Quincy said.

Alex kept his eyes on the video game player, but his thumbs quit moving.

"My turn to count?" I asked. "Or should we do something else?"

Alex bit his lip but still didn't look at me. Before Quincy could answer, I said, "I don't want to seek or hide, actually. I was thinking of climbing my favorite tree. I haven't climbed it at all this summer because of Alex."

"Why because of me?" Alex asked.

"Because I don't want you to get hurt, stupid! That tree's too high. I don't want you all scared."

Quincy laughed, but Alex said, "I wouldn't be scared."

"Quincy," I continued, "did you know Alex is from Arizona? He doesn't understand the woods like we do." I laughed and pointed at Alex. "Cactus boy couldn't climb a real tree even if we showed him how to do it."

"Maybe I don't want to climb it," Alex said.

"Maybe you can't," I said. "Quincy could because he lives here."

"Obviously," Quincy said.

"You're just a tourist," Alex said. He set the game player on the bench and crossed his arms.

"Even though I'm just a tourist, I can do it better than people who live here. I've done it like a million times."

Quincy nodded. "I've done it a million times, too."

"I would have done it a million times if I lived by the woods," Alex said. "I'm not scared of heights."

"But I'm the best climber in my school," I said, "and I bet my school is a million times bigger than your tiny school, Quincy. It'd be easy to be the best climber in a tiny school."

"My school's not tiny!"

I turned to Quincy and put my hands on my hips. "Alex is right. Alex is totally not afraid of heights or anything, really. The school here is so small, Alex probably could climb better than you. And he's from Arizona!"

"I'm not afraid of heights, either. I'm the least afraid ten-year-old ever."

I doubled over laughing. "You're only *ten*? Alex already has a ten-year-old friend. Me! You're small, just like your school. You're too small to teach Alex how to climb a tree."

Quincy stared at Alex. "I'm not small. And my school's not small. And I can climb trees better than a girl or a kid from Arizona."

Alex stared at Quincy. "I don't need you to show me anything. Anyone can climb a dumb tree. Anyone."

"That's right," I said. "Follow me."

I led them to the climbing tree, which was in the woods between our cabin and Westman's boat landing. The tree stood tall and thick, with branches that invited hands and feet. Before turning into Amelia The Princess, my sister had showed me how to climb it: The lowest branch was higher than our heads, so we'd dragged two old wooden crates to the tree and set them against the trunk. She had stood on the crates, grabbed the lowest branch with both hands, and swung her leg onto the branch. She'd pulled herself to a sitting position. I was short, so I had to jump from the crates to grab the tree. While I dangled, she'd pulled on my arms until I could swing my leg up and over. We'd climbed up four branches before Dad found us and made us get down from that tree or else.

The old crates were still there, like nothing had changed even though everything had changed.

"So we have to stand on the crates to reach that branch," I said to Quincy and Alex. "Then it's almost like a staircase. Easy. I suppose I should lead the way since I'm the expert here."

Quincy stepped in front of me. "I'll go first. You go second. Alex can follow you, if he can keep up."

"I'll go first," Alex told Quincy. "You might see a spider and scream like a girl. We have tarantulas in Arizona. Little Wisconsin tree spiders don't scare me."

"I'm not afraid of spiders." Quincy's face looked angry and mean.

I said, "I probably should go last because I'm a little afraid of tree spiders."

Quincy pushed in front of Alex and stood on the crates. With a little jump, he had both hands around the branch. He hooked his leg around it and pulled himself upright. He climbed one more branch and looked down at Alex.

"Hey Alex! You waiting for a ladder?" He laughed.

I laughed, too. "Good one, Quincy!"

Sweat dripped from Alex's face to his shirt. He cleared his throat and stepped on the crates. After a few deep breaths, he grabbed the branch and caught up to Quincy. I came behind both of them. Alex followed Quincy branch by branch, but I stopped and waited on the first branch.

"It's a good thing you're slow, Quincy. Alex can't keep up."

At the same time as Quincy yelled, "I'm not slow," Alex yelled, "I'm keeping up."

I straddled the branch and watched Quincy cross to the thicker branches on the other side of the tree. He climbed another couple of feet and shouted, "That's about as high as the thick branches go. They get too skinny."

"The tallest branches are the strongest because they're the oldest," I yelled. "Just like Alex and you. He's stronger because he's older."

"Is not," Quincy said with a grunt. He climbed a couple more branches. I could barely see him through the leaves. Pretty soon I could barely see Alex, either. I lowered myself back to the crates and jumped to the ground. With all my might I pulled those crates far from the tree.

I heard Alex yell, "Hey! What are you doing?"

"I think I'm going back to the cabin to paint my nails, because I'm just a girl!"

As I ran through the weeds toward the cabin, I plugged my ears so I could honestly say I hadn't heard Alex and his stupid new friend shouting for help.

NEWS AND
FISH

It was decided Alex and I needed some time apart.

Our parents' decision worked out better for Alex than for me. He got to have a "guys' day" with his dad that included riding go-carts in town and playing mini-golf.

But I didn't get to have a guys' day or a girls' day. My parents had to teach. Amelia The Princess had the day off, but she was waterskiing with Matt Fat-Gnat near his house. I had to stay behind with Grumpa, and I was told to avoid all trees.

I sat on the sofa with my arms crossed and watched Grumpa. First, he read the newspaper. Then he turned on the TV. His TV was so old it was shaped like a small box instead of big and flat. His shows were so old they didn't have color. Just black and white and gray like my mood. Outside the sun shined and the lake called to me: *jump! splash! swim!*

During a commercial, Grumpa stood up. "Don't touch my remote or my programs. I'm going to the can."

"What's the can?"

When he stood up, his leg brushed against the table and knocked the newspaper onto the floor. "For the love of Gertrude, the can means the bathroom."

He left the room, and I picked up the newspaper for him. The front page said:

CAPONE'S HIDEAWAY BURGLARIZED AGAIN

Gangster Al Capone's former hideaway near Hayward was burglarized and vandalized last week—the third time in just two years.

Sheriff Tim Duncan said the burglars apparently were looking for money. According to local legend, Capone split up his millions and hid cash in secret locations, including Chicago and Wisconsin's Northwoods. Capone knew he was going to be arrested, and he feared the police and his rivals would get their hands on his fortune.

"The property is no longer open for tours. Nobody lives there. It's a secluded property, so it's ripe for illegal activity," Sheriff Duncan said. "We will add extra patrols in that area."

Duncan said there has been significant damage to the home during the last several years, and nothing of value remains in the house. "It's terrible. These people have ripped up walls and floors. They've dug holes in the ground and torn up the furniture still there."

Capone's hideout sits on 400 acres and includes a house, garages, grounds, and a private lake. The property was once open for tours, but it closed during the economic downturn. Tourists came to the

Northwoods in smaller numbers, erasing profits for Northwoods businesses.

A recent proposal to reopen the property fell through because financing couldn't be secured.

"It's the same old problem out there—crazy people looking for treasure," Duncan said. "It's highly unlikely Capone hid money in the house. If he did, it was found long ago."

There was a handwritten note on the newspaper that said,

> Ed—Here's the article I told you about. What's going on out there? I guess Duncan's on the case—HAH!
>
> Walt

Mr. Walt Miller! That old fart was nosy! I wondered if he'd seen the hole behind the washtub in Grumpa's basement. I remembered the day he brought tools to fix the pipes. He'd told Grumpa that Sheriff Duncan had stopped him near Capone's hideout. He'd driven the longest possible way to get to Grumpa's from Hayward, supposedly because of tourist traffic. That was crazy—there wasn't much traffic outside of town and hardly any around Westman Drive. Mr. Walt Miller was lying, and I knew why. He was after the Clarks' cash.

I picked up the remote to make room on the table for the newspaper, and that's when Grumpa returned from the can.

"I told you not to touch that remote!" Grumpa yelled. "Hell's bells! Is it possible for you to sit still for ten minutes?"

I'd been asked this question before but never in such a loud voice. His voice was so loud my eyes were starting to sweat.

"For the love of Gertrude, don't cry!"

I pressed my lips together so no sounds would come out. I plopped on the sofa and folded my arms.

"For the love of Gertrude." Grumpa shifted around in his recliner and turned up the volume.

The commercials stopped and his stupid show started again. Stupid show. Stupid grumpy Grumpa. I used my t-shirt to soak up my eye sweats.

Grumpa sighed all big and pressed buttons to turn down the sound. "Minnow, I suppose you want me to entertain you."

I shrugged.

"I've been meaning to wash my truck. I could watch you do it. I'd have to make sure you don't drown yourself with the hose."

"No thanks."

He turned the TV off and put the footrest down. "I got some fish on ice that need to be scaled and cleaned. We could do that."

"Can I use the knife?"

"That's all I need. You cutting off your leg. Or worse, cutting off my leg!"

If he wouldn't let me use a knife, there was no point in asking if he'd teach me taxidermy.

He said, "I could show you how to make pizza dough. It's soft and squishy. So you could squish it around for a while."

"Then can I have a job at the restaurant?"

"No."

"I don't want to squish dough."

Grumpa said, "Fine. Tell me what you want to do."

A few minutes later, we were zipping across Whitefish Lake in Grumpa's speedboat. And I was steering! Grumpa kept his hand on his hat so it wouldn't blow away. The wind dried the sweat on my face, and lake water sprayed the sides of the boat. I let my right hand dangle in the mist while I steered with my left. I shrieked and turned the wheel right and then left so the boat cut through the water in the path of a corkscrew.

"Enough!" Grumpa yelled over the rumbling motor. He reached over and pulled the lever. The boat went from a zip to a chug. "You can head to the cove on the east side, the one past the sandbar. That's enough speeding for one day. My ticker doesn't like it." He thumped his chest.

I knew the place because I'd seen Grumpa fishing there every summer. I steered slowly to the cove. Grumpa dropped the anchor into the water with a *plunk*. "You can use that pole, but I'm not hooking your bait. You're gonna have to touch worms."

"I'm not afraid of worms or hooking them. I'm not afraid of anything except sharks and maybe snakes a little."

Grumpa handed me the container of worms. I pulled out the fattest one I could find and rolled it in my hand just to show him how unafraid I was. Then I stretched it over the hook. In a swift move my arm arched back and flicked the line into the water. Like a professional.

Grumpa cast his line, too.

I wanted to show him I was a real fisherperson, but it was hard to be quiet and still as the lake. I couldn't sit on my hands because I had to hold the pole. My teacher had told me to count to fifty before I say or do things. She said counting was a strategy to make me think first, but actually her strategy just made me a very fast counter.

Before I got to fifty, Grumpa reeled in his line.

I hadn't even noticed his bobber dart under the water. He pulled out a tiny perch and shook his head all disgusted. "Look at this." He unhooked the perch and dropped it in the water. "Too many people fishing in this lake these days. I swear you used to get fifteen-pound walleyes every time you put bait in the water. There's just too much lake property being bought up, and it's being bought by people who don't respect the lake."

"Like people who need fancy fishing radars to catch anything," I grumped.

"Gerald Westman—that's the guy who built your cabin—owned a lot of lake property. He made a fortune selling it. Now we've got people here who overfish and don't know how properly to get rid of fish guts. Last week I caught a tourist dumping minnows in the water. Don't they know that's how we get non-native fish in our lakes?"

I shook my head. "They don't know anything!"

After I counted to fifty, I asked, "Is that why

you don't want us to sell my cabin? Because we respect the lake and the new people probably won't?"

"Who said I don't want you to sell it?"

"Alex said you'd rather have us next to you even though I'm a pain."

"That kid! Words go in his ear and straight out his mouth."

I reeled in my line to make sure a fish hadn't nibbled my worm. I hadn't felt a single tug. The worm, now gray and bloated, still clung to the hook. I cast the line again. "Grumpa, did you help build Al Capone's hideout?"

"Hell's bells! How old do you think I am?"

"I saw that newspaper article from Mr. Walt Miller in the living room. Do you think he's after Capone's stash?"

"Walt? That old fart would take a dime from an orphan."

"Grumpa, would you tell me the rest of the story? The part after Al Capone gave your dad some of his fortune?"

Grumpa sighed.

"Please? If you don't want to, we could talk about something else. We could make a list of the ten best things about Hayward."

"If it's a choice between having to listen to you or listen to myself, I guess I might as well finish the story."

AL CAPONE AND THE CLARK FAMILY LOOT

Al Capone's brain was rotting from his disease. He had enough wits, though, to realize he was going to get caught, and his fortune would end up with the government or his enemies. He didn't like either outcome. Capone started hiding money. He gave some of it to his buddies to keep safe while he was in prison.

Most of his buddies were too scared of Capone to run off with his money. They did what he asked. But others figured Capone wouldn't survive prison. They figured if he did survive prison, he'd be a nothing when he got out. There'd be new gangsters, and Capone's days of ruling Chicago were over. Those buddies not only decided to keep his money, but they figured they'd steal from each other.

As soon as my father got home with that suitcase of money, trouble came looking for it—trouble named Johnny Russo and Sammy Costa. They were as mean as Capone.

I was sleeping in my bedroom upstairs when Johnny and Sammy came looking for the suitcase. I woke up to a commotion. Yelling and cussing. I looked from my window and saw Johnny and Sammy had my dad outside. I knew them from the restaurant. Sometimes they ate with Capone.

Sammy held Pops down and Johnny slapped him around. It was terrible to see such a thing. Pops was so tough. But not that night. I was real little and there was nothing I could do.

My mother—my tiny church-going mother—came out of the house with a rifle and stood at the driveway. Now my old man brewed his own trouble, but my mother was a wonderful woman, and I was scared out of my pants that something might happen to her.

She said, "That money's not here. I'm a Christian woman, and there's no room for blood money in my home or my heart. That money is the devil's calling card."

I knew that suitcase full of money was hidden in a crate in the basement. My folks had been fighting about it all week. My mother said she was going to give it to the police, and my father threatened to hurt her if she touched it.

Pops tried to tear himself away from Sammy and Johnny, yelling that he didn't have any of Capone's money. They smacked him again and told him to shut up and that they didn't believe him.

Then my mother held the rifle to her eye. She said, "I don't care if you believe me or not. You gotta get through me to get to him. You going to kill a woman in cold blood? In the Northwoods? People here know who you are and what you are. This isn't Chicago where you can get away with killing. If you hurt me, folks here will hang you."

They seemed to think about that. I just hoped Pops would keep his big mouth shut and let my mother take care of this mess. Then she said, "Now if I shoot you, two gangsters from the city, gangsters who come to my home and threaten my family, I'm a hero and a saint. They'll build a statue of me in the park, and your own mothers won't shed a tear at your funerals because you're bad men."

Sammy said, "You couldn't hit the side of a barn with that rifle."

My mother said, "I can hit the side of a birdhouse with this rifle." And she fired a shot. In the moon-light, you could see the birdhouse near the very end of the driveway blow into a thousand pieces. I couldn't believe it. I didn't know my mother could even hold a gun. That was a one-in-a-million shot.

Then she said, "Your heads make a fine and easy target."

Sure enough, they backed away, got in their car, and they sped out of there.

The next day, she got a bottle of whiskey and said my father deserved a nice drink after a night like that. He should've been suspicious. I was. But he started drinking. Pretty soon he'd passed right out. That's when my mother sent me to my room and said to stay there while she hid the money where nobody would find it, including my father. I guess that's when she put it in the basement under the washtub.

When Pops woke up, she wouldn't tell him where she'd hid the money. She said he wasn't going to drink and gamble it away. She said they were either going to do good things with that money or get rid of it. He was burning mad. I thought he was going to hit her, but she said, "If it weren't for Edmund, I'd have let those thugs take you. If I can shoot a bird-house from the other end of the driveway, imagine what I can do while you're sleeping. Close range and all."

So he never hit her. And they never, not once, spoke another word to each other. Not at home, not at the restaurant. Not ever. My father died a few months later, and misfortune started raining down. Mother kept talking about us burning that money together, but then she'd change her mind and talk about who she could help. Then she'd say she was afraid to give the money to the church. She thought bad things would happen to the pastor. She was afraid to give the money to the orphanage because she thought bad things would happen to the kids. She thought if Capone got the money back, the curse would lift, but he was in prison. She thought maybe after Capone died, the curse would lift, but she decided she couldn't wait. The loot had to go. She said she was going to burn it up.

That whole time, she never let me have a penny of that money. I thought I might get a train set out of the deal, but no. Couldn't even get one little train set, and trains were my favorite thing in the world. We ran the restaurant and worked day and night. My mother wanted me to understand an honest dollar. There was no tree climbing, no running around, no train collecting, and no swinging from water pipes in the basement, that's for darn sure.

So the Clark family loot came to an end with a match and a fire.

"That's it? That's the end?"

"That's it, Minnow."

The whole story was a sad mess. All that money and she burned it? She wouldn't even give her kid a train set? That's crazy. Mrs. Hillary Clark could have made it so Grumpa didn't have to work so hard, and then Grumpa could have made it so Neil didn't have to work so hard. Their lives could've been easier and happier.

One match took everything from the Clarks.

It took something from me, too. After Dad had cried and Shawn Weller's sign had gone in the yard, I mostly knew the cabin was gone. Still, I'd had the teeny-tiniest piece of hope that Capone's money might save the cabin. It wasn't big hope. It was speck-of-dust hope, but now even that was gone. How could losing something so small feel so big and empty?

"Stories don't have happy endings, Minnow." Grumpa said. "You'll save yourself a lot of grief if you stop looking for them."

I didn't feel like fishing anymore. I reeled in my

line, yanked the bloated worm off the hook, and dropped it in the water. A few sunfish darted to the surface and nibbled until the worm was gone.

"I've got some golden shiners," Grumpa said. "Want to try one?"

"No thanks." I leaned back in my seat and studied the shoreline. If I squinted I could make out the shape of the Clarks' house from our fishing spot.

Grumpa looked toward the house, too, and said, "I've always wondered where she burned it."

"You didn't see her burn it?"

"Didn't need to."

I sat up so fast I knocked my fishing pole over. "Then you're not sure."

"She said she was going to. That's good enough for me." Grumpa lifted his fishing hat and wiped sweat from his forehead.

"But you didn't see it with your own eyes!"

"Look, my mother was convinced about the curse. The whole time we hid the money, it just brought on God's wrath."

"What exactly happened?"

"My father dropped dead from a heart attack. He died so fast he still had his fingers wrapped around a whiskey bottle when they found him. A storm ripped the roof off our house. We had a kitchen fire at the restaurant. My uncle nearly drowned. This whole area was hit by drought." Grumpa coughed and gross things rattled in his chest. He sighed. "She wanted to do something good with it, but she was afraid. She changed her mind about that money at least once a day. It tore her up."

"So one day she just says to you, 'I burned the money.'"

"Well, she said she didn't know what to do and she didn't want to burden me and she thought it'd be best if she'd burned it."

"She *thought*? Or she *did*?"

"Hell's bells!"

"You're not sure, are you?"

"I didn't see it with my own eyes, but she said she did."

Grumpa reeled in his line. His bait was gone—snatched from the hook without his noticing. He opened the Styrofoam container and plucked a worm from the dirt. His thick fingers threaded the worm onto the hook. With a stretch, he cast his line back into the water.

"Grumpa, I have this feeling," I said. "I don't think she actually burned the money."

He grunted and shook his head.

"If she thought there was a way to make the curse lift without burning the money, don't you think she would've tried it?"

"If she did, she kept it a secret, and she took the secret to her grave."

I wondered what Mrs. Hillary Clark might have been thinking and feeling. Every time she made a steak at the restaurant, was she thinking about Capone and her husband and her son? Was she thinking about how much easier life was before that suitcase showed up and changed everything?

I was going to say these things to Grumpa, but he was staring into the water. His eyes were soft, lost in thought and memories so deep he didn't notice a fish tugging his bobber under the water.

That night I woke to the sound of sniffles. I dropped my head over the side of the bunk. From upside down I saw Amelia propped up on pillows, crying.

"What's wrong?" I whispered.

Amelia dabbed her tears with the sheet. "You wouldn't understand."

"Maybe I would."

"It's complicated."

"You woke me up. You might as well tell me."

She sighed. "Fine, but I can't talk with your face hanging upside down like that."

I rolled over, jumped down, and sat on the edge of her bunk. She let out a sob. "It's the cabin! I can't believe Mom and Dad are selling it."

I thought I must be dreaming. Amelia cared about the cabin, and she was wiping her nose with the sheet, like she used to do, instead of getting up and looking for a tissue. Amelia My Sister!

"Maybe we should try talking to them together. Our tag-team thing we do," Amelia said. "Then they'd have to listen."

Weeks ago—even a few days ago—Amelia's plan would've been brilliant. That was before I'd seen my dad cry and Grumpa's faraway eyes.

"We could, but . . . I don't know. Mom and Dad are feeling pretty bad," I said.

"What? I don't get it. I thought you'd do anything to save the cabin."

"I thought you hated the cabin."

"Hate it? Are you crazy? If we sell the cabin, I'll never get to see Matt again!" Then she started to blubber cry.

Matt? Matt Cat-Brat? "So what? You can text him, can't you?"

"You can't have a real relationship through a phone, Christa. You don't get it." She sounded annoyed. "He's so sweet. He's always helping me keep up with my tables at the restaurant. He keeps an eye on my tips because there's this waiter we think is stealing."

"That's nice. We need the money."

"Then there's that play date he helped arrange with his cousin Quincy. He cares about Alex having a real friend. That's how sweet he is."

I guess I was too tired to talk, because there were no words in my head except *real friend*. A *real friend* for Alex, thanks to Amelia's sweet boyfriend. Was I driving Alex crazy the way I'd driven Amelia crazy? Was I not a real friend?

"Oh." That's all I said.

"Never mind. Just go to sleep. You'll understand this stuff when you're older."

I was still growing too slow.

FISH AND
VISITORS

More than anything, I wanted to tell Alex about
the loot and how his great-grandmother didn't burn
it, maybe. But I didn't know if we were still friends,
and I didn't get a chance to find out. My parents
decided to keep us apart one more day since Amelia
didn't have to work.

Instead of sending me to Grumpa's, they told
her to go fishing with me. As soon as they left for
work, she got out her phone and invited Matt Pat-
That and his buddy Travis to join us.

Four people casting lines at the end of the dock

doesn't work. There are too many hooks in the air. Didn't matter, though, because the only things Amelia The Princess wanted to catch were princes. Travis seemed to like Amelia as much as Matt, and Amelia seemed to know it and love it. Matt and Travis were tripping over each other in a war of charm.

"I haven't fished in years," Amelia said. Her mini-shorts showed off tan legs, and her hair was pulled into a messy bun, like she'd spent only two seconds twisting her golden locks into a band. Actually she needed a half hour in front of a mirror, plus gel and hairspray, to make her hair look like that.

"Want me to bait your hook?" Travis asked.

"I just did my nails so, yes, thanks."

Travis blushed as he said, "Why don't you fish from the lawn chair? Then you don't have to stand."

"I've got the worms," Matt said. "I'll hook her up."

Amelia smiled as she relaxed in the lawn chair.

Matt and Travis reached down to get the

container of night crawlers. In their clumsy wrestle, the container fell, scattering dirt and worms across the dock. A couple of worms dropped into the lake, making a hook-free meal for some fish.

I got on my knees and scraped the contents back into the container. I held one worm between my thumb and finger and waved it hypnotist style in front of Amelia's face. "You are getting very sleepy!"

"Get that worm away from my face!" She smacked my arm.

"Get your face away from my worm!"

Travis nabbed the worm from my fingers. "I've got it."

While I fished, Amelia, Matt, and Travis swapped stories about working at Clarks Pizza. I tried to ignore them. The buzz of deer flies was more interesting than their stories.

Grumpa and Alex walked down the slope with their fishing gear. Grumpa nodded hello as they set up their gear at the end of their dock, which was about thirty feet from ours. I yelled, "Hi!" but Alex didn't answer. He didn't even look at me.

Alex was holding a different fishing pole, a new pole. They weren't far away, but a fishing pole is very skinny. I dug through the bag with our gear and pulled out Dad's old binoculars. I kneeled next to Amelia and peeked around her chair with the binoculars.

Amelia stopped talking to the boys. "Christa, what are you doing?"

"Bird watching."

She rolled her eyes and continued her story about a cook who covered a pizza with peppers instead of pepperoni.

With the binoculars I could see Alex holding a hunter green WildPro Rod and Reel, classic series. Grumpa had bought him a new fishing pole, and not just any old pole. The WildPro Rod and Reel had a graphite core coated in fiberglass. I'd seen them in Nan's shop. I remembered the packaging as though it were in front of me. *The WildPro Rod and Reel offers greater control, fewer tangles, and superior performance.*

And here I was with my stinky old Struken rod-and-reel combo. Alex was too stupid to know the difference between a WildPro and a Struken. Alex couldn't even tell the difference between bobber movements, whether the line had snagged a fish or weeds.

Grumpa put one hand on Alex's shoulder and the other on his arm, showing Alex how to swing back the line and snap it forward. The bobber landed with a plop about five feet away. I heard Grumpa say, "Not bad, kid. Let your wrist do the work. Your arm's just a guide."

From the shore a voice called, "Let go of the button just as you snap your wrist!" I was about to yell the same thing, but Neil had said it first. He'd been standing on shore. Slowly he walked down the dock. He stood a few feet behind them, watching Alex get casting lessons from Grumpa.

Travis's voice got my attention. In a whisper he was telling Amelia, "You're so lucky you didn't have to work for him. Such a crackpot."

Then Matt Spat-Gnat whispered, "There's a walk-in freezer in the basement from when they used to serve steaks and fancy food. That's where he hides money. He doesn't trust banks."

"So he trusts cheap padlocks and an ancient freezer but not a bank?" Amelia snorted.

Travis quietly laughed. "Ed Clark hangs on to his money tighter than a leech on a dog's belly."

I wanted to push all three of them in the lake. "Stop it! You're mean!"

"Keep it down," Amelia said. "They'll hear you."

"Stop talking about them and their money. You don't know anything about it."

Matt cocked his eyebrow. "Oh, and you do?"

"Christa spends a lot of time with the Clarks." Amelia shot me a shut-up-or-else look. "Maybe too much time."

Matt asked, "What have the Clarks been telling you?"

I mumbled, "Nothing."

"Come on, Christa." Matt spoke slowly, like I was a baby. "We aren't going to tell anyone. It's not like we'd steal his money. We're just curious, that's all."

"He said if anyone touches his money, he'll cut off their fingers and use the tips for bait."

Amelia sort of waved me away with her hand and started talking about a mean customer. I looked at Alex. He pulled his pole back and released the line in a perfect arc. Grumpa clapped and called out, "You're a heck of a student!"

I yelled, "You're a heck of a teacher, Grumpa!"

Neil nodded. I swear he even smiled.

That evening, a car drove up to the Clarks' house. I pulled down the blinds on the window so I could watch through the slats without being seen. Parents and two boys got out of the car.

One boy looked exactly Alex's age. The other was younger. Neil and the parents talked while the boys ran toward the lake.

Dad touched my shoulder. "What's up, sweetie?"

"Who are those people?"

"That's Nan's son, daughter-in-law, and her grandkids. Nan arranged for them to visit so Alex could meet some kids from school. Neil and Sally want him to make some friends before school starts."

I dropped to the couch and crossed my arms. Suddenly Nan felt like a traitor. "He's being a huge baby. It was just a stupid tree."

"Alex is a nervous kid. He was scared, Christa. I know Alex and Quincy were being mean to you, and that's not okay, but the difference between what they did to you and what you did to them has an important distinction. They could've been hurt, physically hurt. Do you understand?"

"I do. But it seems like nobody wants us to be friends anymore."

"That's not the case. You both needed time to think. Tomorrow is probably the time for apologies, okay? You're still friends. I'm sure of it."

Mom poked her head out of the bedroom. "Everyone get ready. We're going out for pizza. Shawn Weller is bringing some people to look at the cabin, so we need to clear out."

AN APOLOGY AND
ANOTHER APOLOGY

For the first time ever, Clarks Pizza was the worst place in Hayward and in the world, basically. Shawn Weller was selling our cabin while my family huddled around a big pepperoni pizza. Every time I wanted to cross my arms and pout, I stopped myself. I thought about my parents crying, how sad they'd been, how Dad blamed himself.

I'd swallowed so much sadness there was no room for pizza.

Mom asked, "Why aren't you girls eating?"

I shrugged while Amelia typed into her phone

like she hadn't heard Mom. Dad clutched her arm. "Put that down and eat with your family, please."

Her sigh was big like a hurricane. She put the phone on the table and picked up a fork. Amelia poked her pizza but didn't eat.

Dad asked, "What's wrong?"

"Doesn't matter," she said. "Nobody cares."

Now Dad sighed. "What?"

"Nothing."

"Amelia, clearly something is bothering you. What is it?"

"Am I the only person who cares about selling the cabin? I finally made friends up here. Years and years of not knowing a single person, just Christa, and now I meet these cool people from the restaurant and I'll never see them again." There were princess tears in her princess eyes.

"I'm sorry about your friends, Amelia," Dad said.

Mom nodded. "We're sorry, honey. We are. But you can stay in touch online, and you can invite them to visit us at home."

"Why'd they want to come to our stupid town? There aren't any lakes or woods or anything special. Am I supposed to take them to a *mall*? God, Mom, you just don't get it."

Amelia slid her plate across the table in a huff. Mom and Dad looked like they'd been smacked. They looked tired and sad and sick of everything.

"It's not all about you, Amelia. Maybe you could do us a favor and grow up." I pulled a napkin from the dispenser and placed it in her lap. "Does anyone else need a napkin?"

Dad blinked a couple times. I think he was waiting for me to throw the napkin in Amelia's face, but I didn't. I gave a napkin to Dad.

"Thanks, Christa."

Mom's phone rang. "Hello? Oh, hi Shawn. How'd it go? . . . hmm . . . and what'd you say? . . . hmm . . . I see. Thank you for the update."

I was afraid to hear her report. Bad news would be a sale. Bad news also would be no sale and my parents looking weighed down by their bills.

"What'd he say?" Dad asked.

Mom took a deep breath. "He said the boy from next door told them the cabin was infested with so many bats that his family couldn't sit outside at night. He told them the roof was falling in, and we were keeping it upright with bungee cords."

Everyone looked at me.

"I didn't tell him to say those things. I swear!" I felt both anger and awe. "Sometimes I say I didn't do something wrong, and I even swear that I didn't do it, but I did. That's not what I'm doing right now. I double triple swear I never never never never asked Alex to say those things. I don't want you to have all those bills and maybe lose our house and our cars and be homeless."

My eyes filled with sweat. Mom kissed the top of my head. "I believe you, honey."

Dad reached across the table, gave my fist a squeeze, and said, "Don't worry, Christa. We're not going to lose our house. We're not going to be homeless. It's fine. Mom and I will always make sure you're taken care of, right?"

"Absolutely." Mom put on a big smile. "This is just a bump in the road. Everything will be fine."

"Maybe there will be a miracle, and we'll get a bunch of money," I said.

"We don't need a miracle. Things will be fine without any miracles." Dad used the word "fine" again. That's what made me think we *did* need a miracle.

I took a bite of my pizza to make them feel better and said, "Why would Alex say those things?"

"Close your mouth when you chew," Amelia said. Then she smiled. "Alex said those things because he likes you and doesn't want you to leave, dummy."

I thought about Alex and Quincy and Nan's grandsons, boys who might be real friends. "You're the dummy, Amelia."

For once, I hoped she wasn't.

That night, just as I closed my eyes, there was a tap, tap, tap on the window screen. I sprang up and saw Alex peeking in the window. Our bedroom window was long, but narrow, and set high in the wall. My bunk was almost pressed against it.

"What are you doing?" I whispered even though I wanted to shout from the excitement of seeing him.

"I'm on a step stool trying to wake you up."

I tipped my head upside down to check Amelia's bunk. She looked asleep. She wore earbuds and listened to music while she slept. I popped up and pressed my nose against the screen.

"Okay. I'm awake."

He was quiet for a long time. "A person would have to be pretty mean to trick a friend into climbing something too tall."

"The old hide-and-never-seek is pretty mean, too."

He said, "Maybe I'm sorry."

I said, "Maybe I'm sorry, too."

We stayed nose-to-nose. I heard a buzz, and Alex slapped a mosquito on his forehead.

"Maybe I'm wondering if those boys who came

over tonight were any fun." I said it like I didn't care about his answer.

"Maybe they were fun and way nicer than Quincy and maybe one of them is in my grade. So what?"

"So now you've got two new friends, and I guess those are all the friends you need." I crossed my arms.

Alex slapped another mosquito and scraped it off his cheek with his fingernail. "Maybe it's good to have extra friends because the friend who's the most fun doesn't even live here."

His words stopped all the bad feelings.

"Oh," I said. "That makes sense."

"Well, that's all I wanted."

"You could've told me this in the morning."

"Sometimes I can't sleep when I'm thinking about stuff. I figured I'd stop thinking about it if I just, you know, did something. So I did and now I'm done. I'll see you tomorrow, okay?"

"Wait!" I smacked the screen. "I have so much to

tell you. I asked Grumpa about the loot. Your great-grandma wanted to burn it because it was cursed, but Grumpa isn't sure if she did. He says she was always wondering if the curse would lift when Capone died. So I'm thinking, what if she returned it to Capone's hideout to stop the curse?"

"You think she gave it back?"

"Maybe she thought she could have it both ways. She could stop the curse by hiding the loot at Capone's. It was like giving it back, right? Then she waited for Capone to die. If the curse died with Capone, she could go get the money later."

"But then she died before Capone."

"Exactly! Alex, do you think we could find it? Because I do."

"Me, too. I think we could."

"We'll split the money."

"Fifty-fifty. Finders keepers, Christa. We'll be the finders and the keepers." Alex held up his hand, and I gave him a soft high five against the screen. "Tomorrow we go to Capone's."

Alex got off the step stool, folded it, and dragged it across the lawn.

I pulled the sheet up to my chin and thought about finding the loot. My parents would pay all our bills and take down Shawn Weller's sign. There was a second plan, too. When we found all that cash, I was going to buy Grumpa his very own train set.

TRUSTED AND
BUSTED

Alex and I waited for Grumpa to take his nap
in the recliner. We had to search Al Capone's hideout for the loot, and we didn't have much time.
When you're doing something you're not supposed
to do, you need to do it *fast*. Torpedo fast.

That's why we didn't ride our bikes. We took
the ATV.

We had helmets hiding our faces, so none of the
people in cars seemed to notice we were young.
Nobody honked or slowed down. We zipped
through ditches and along the shoulder of the road,

spitting gravel into the air. After we passed the gas station, Alex turned on the road that led to the hide-out. The trees stretched across the road and formed a canopy. Weeds and brush were so thick along the ditch I couldn't see through the woods. A barb-wire fence bordered the land. As we got closer to a lone driveway with a gate across it, I tapped Alex's shoulder.

The ATV spurted and stopped. "You sure this is it?" he asked. "There aren't any signs. I can't see a house or anything through these woods."

"I'm sure. I used Amelia's phone to look it up. They took down the signs to keep people away."

"Guess they didn't take down everything." Alex pointed to a tree. A sign nailed in the trunk said, *Private property. Trespassers will be prosecuted.*

"Do you think the law respects the finders-keepers rule?"

Alex took off his helmet. "First things first. We can't keep unless we *find*."

We belly crawled under the gate and took a few careful steps. The trees grew tight along the sides of the driveway, which took a sharp turn to the right. Our feet crunched against the gravel as we followed the crooked path. There wasn't any traffic, and we weren't goofing around, but in the woods even quiet is loud. Squirrels rustled the weeds. Cicadas buzzed and clicked. Chirping birds seemed to scold us from the trees.

"How far do you think it is?" Alex wondered.

"He had a lot of land. There's a private lake in here. The driveway could be really, really long."

"Tons of adults have already searched this place. They've looked in all the obvious spots. We have to think different, think like Chase and Buck. We have to look in the places nobody else thought about." I wasn't used to Alex—or Buck—taking charge. Chase and I were the charge-takers. He continued, "For starters, we need to look behind all the sinks."

"Right. If your great-grandmother hid money in the wall behind the sink at your house, she might have done the same thing here."

The driveway curved around a group of pine

trees. Alex's careful steps turned into marching. "We've got to hurry. Grandpa will get up soon."

"But he won't start looking for us right away," I said. "Not for an hour at least. Maybe longer. Have you noticed he's not that interested in what we're up to?"

"Grandpa thinks we can take care of ourselves. My dad says Grandpa thinks kids are just little adults." Alex stopped speaking and walking. "Did you hear that?"

"What?"

"Like something on the gravel."

Then I heard it, too. The crunch of footsteps. I whirled around, but the pine trees blocked my view. Alex and I stopped, eyes big and shoulders tight. I grabbed his arm, and we darted into the brush and dropped to our bellies behind a fallen tree.

Alex's breath was coming hard and fast. I couldn't see over the log without lifting my head and giving away our hiding spot. I made a Chase-like move, rolling to the end of the fallen tree where the roots fanned out like spindly fingers. Carpenter ants, black and fat and as long as my thumbnail, scattered across the rotting trunk. I looked at Alex. His eyes were screwed shut.

A deep voice called, "Show yourself!"

I peeked through the roots. I could see black shoes and black pants, but his body was hidden by brush and a wide pine tree. The shoes moved two steps forward, and his hand came out from behind the pine tree. In his hand was a gun.

I stretched my leg toward Alex and gave him a kick to get his attention. When he opened his eyes, I put my thumb up and my pointer finger out, making the shape of a gun. He looked like he wanted to melt into the ground and disappear.

Once more I peeked through the roots. The man moved a few more feet, clearing the pine tree and stepping into the sunlight. A police officer. Sheriff Duncan. Every muscle in my body relaxed.

I mouthed the words to Alex: "Sheriff Duncan."

"I've got the license plate off the ATV," the sheriff shouted. "Show yourself now. I'll track down the licensed owner in my computer and then we'll have real trouble."

Chase Truegood and Buck Punch would never surrender, but Chase and Buck weren't getting busted using an ATV with a licensed owner named Mr. Edmund Clark.

Alex raised his eyebrows at me. I raised mine back. He took a few breaths and cleared his throat. He squeaked, "Over here."

Sheriff Duncan's head whipped toward us. "Stand up, slow and careful. Keep your hands up."

Slow and careful we got to our knees, and then to our feet, with our hands pointing straight in the air. Sheriff Duncan shook his head and slipped his gun into its holster.

"Get out of the weeds. Now."

We slopped through the brush, arms still in the air, and stood in front of him.

"Put your arms down." His voice rumbled. "You're the kids from the bait shop. Alex Clark. What are you looking for out here, Alex Clark?"

The sheriff didn't seem interested in me at all, and for once I was okay not being noticed. "You're the second batch of trespassers I've chased out of here today. Couldn't catch the first, but they were teenagers. They run fast." Teenagers? My mind went straight to Matt Fat-Splat and his buddy Travis. Matt was one step ahead of us. "Does your grandpa know you're out here looking for something? Did he send you?"

Alex shook his head.

"Listen, kid, your family's had enough trouble with Capone. I've lived here my entire life and know all about it. If there's something you know about Capone, you need to tell the authorities. Understand?"

Alex nodded.

Sheriff Duncan stared hard at Alex. He cleared his throat and said, "I saw the ATV. You have to be older than twelve *and* with an adult to be out on a road with an ATV. Did you know that?" Alex didn't have time to shrug because Sheriff Duncan kept talking. "Do you know how much trouble you could be in for trespassing? This is private property—"

Alex puked. Right then and right there. Right on Sheriff Duncan's shoes. The birds seemed to stop singing and stare at us. I cleared my throat and said, "Alex gets sick when he's really, really sorry."

I'd always wanted to ride in a police car, but not like a criminal. Sheriff Duncan took us straight to Grumpa's. Alex and I sat on Grumpa's porch swing, quieter than two cotton balls rubbing together, while Grumpa leaned against Sheriff Duncan's car and talked to him through the window.

They talked and talked and stared at us all concerned. Finally, Sheriff Duncan's car backed out of the driveway, and Grumpa marched toward us.

"What in the unholy firestorms of hell were you doing at Capone's old place? What made you think you could take the ATV off this property? Do you know how lucky you are Duncan brought you here instead of writing tickets and dragging you to jail? Duncan hands out tickets like candy on Halloween." Grumpa's eyes were ice. "What were you doing out there?"

Alex confessed. "Looking for Capone's loot."

"Looking for loot? Hell's bells." Grumpa pulled the fishing hat off his head and swatted the air. He stomped his foot, too, and sputtered. He opened the door to the house and let it slam behind him. I figured this is what an old person's temper tantrum looked like.

Thirty minutes later, we were still sitting on Grumpa's porch swing, too scared to get up, when Mr. Walt Miller's car pulled into the driveway. Grumpa stepped outside and waved at him.

Mr. Walt Miller got out of the car, gave a salute, and flashed his creepy smile. "At your service, Ed. Always ready to help a Clark in trouble. Because there's always a Clark in trouble." Grumpa scowled, but Mr. Walt Miller laughed.

Grumpa turned to us and said, "He's taking me out to get that ATV. You stay put. I don't care if a tornado siren goes off. I don't care if Godzilla comes out of the woods. I don't care if an asteroid hits the Earth. Don't leave this porch."

We nodded.

Grumpa barked, "Christa!"

"Yes?"

"What are you going to do if Godzilla comes out of the woods?"

"Don't leave the porch."

He yelled, "Alex!"

"Yes?"

"What are you going to do if you see an asteroid in the sky coming right at your head?"

"Don't leave the porch."

Grumpa grumped his way to Mr. Walt Miller's pickup. They disappeared in a cloud of dust.

I said, "I don't like the looks of that Mr. Walt Miller."

"He looks creepy, but he must be okay. My dad said Walt Miller offered to come here and attach the washtub to the wall."

"That snoop! He's looking for the money."

"I wondered about that. Old Walt said he'd fix the washtub when Grandpa is out fishing so it'd be a surprise. A surprise! He must think we're stupid."

"He just wants to be down there alone so he can hunt for clues."

"Walt told my dad that Grandpa isn't feeling so good, but Grandpa is too proud to let anyone else fix it. That's why Walt wants to surprise him."

That Mr. Walt Miller was slicker than a water slide. He'd probably been sniffing around Capone's, too. He couldn't outrun Sheriff Duncan like a teenager, but he could probably outsmart him.

"So what's next?"

"Amelia's friends think there might be something in a freezer in the basement of the restaurant."

"Why would my great-grandmother move money from the house to the restaurant? They owned both places. One isn't any safer than the other."

"Anyway, Matt and Travis said the freezer is locked. Are there any old keys lying around the house?"

Alex scratched the side of his head. The helmet had left his hair damp and plastered flat against his head. "I've never seen any unusual keys. Just regular keys."

An engine rumbled, and Grumpa arrived on the ATV. He struggled to lift his leg and swing it off the bike. If we were closer, I think we could've heard his body creak. He limped to the porch. "All right. Get inside."

We got inside. Alex and I sat at the kitchen table and waited for instructions.

"This is how things are going to be," Grumpa said. "You're going to stop this nonsense. All this talk about Capone and that money is making me crazy. I don't need to be living in the past. It's bad for the brain when you're old. You two are going to stay out of Sheriff Duncan's sight. He's got no appetite for funny business. Understand?"

We nodded.

"Hell's bells, I should tell your parents, but lucky for you I'm in a good mood. I'm going easy on you this time. I worked my whole life and I'm not giving up my naps and I'm not selling that ATV and you two are not going to get me fired from the job of knowing my grandson."

Grumpa walked to the living room and turned on the TV.

Not tell our parents? Grumpa was the best baby-sitter in the world, mostly.

THE HOLIDAY
AND THE SCARE

Independence Day is the best holiday of all the holidays without presents and egg hunts and birthday cakes. And my parents were trying to ruin it.

"We don't have a lot of money, but we want to do something special for the Fourth of July." Dad set plates on the table for breakfast while Mom flipped pancakes. "We thought we could spend next weekend in Duluth going through the museums."

"We'll get a hotel with a pool!" Mom said.

"It'll be a treat," Dad said. "There's a museum about the logging industry and one about the shipping industry. Then there's a museum dedicated to actress Judy Garland. Remember *The Wizard of Oz*? Well, she was from this area! Wouldn't it be amazing if they have her journals there? I'd love to read her deepest secrets."

We needed to act fast. Faster-than-fast fast. I looked at Amelia, who started tapping on her phone. This was no time to be texting.

"We'll have ice cream!" Mom said.

Amelia turned her phone toward me. She hadn't been texting. She'd typed a note: *Tag team! Follow me.*

"That's so cool!" Amelia said. Then she sighed all big.

Dad asked, "What's the matter, honey?"

"Nothing. I'm glad we'll have a family weekend. I'll just tell all my new friends I can't go."

Mom put a plate of pancakes on the table. "Go where?"

"Travis is having a cookout and everyone's water-skiing and tubing and doing fireworks. No big deal, really."

"I didn't know you'd been invited to a party," Mom said.

"It's the one thing I've been happy about, you know, since it's the last holiday we'll ever have at the cabin. But the museum trip will be pleasant." Amelia never used the word "pleasant."

"Pleasant," I agreed. "Alex wants to have a cook-out and bonfire, too. But maybe we'll get invited next year. Maybe."

Dad's shoulders started to droop. "The city of Duluth has wonderful fireworks. People come from all over to see them."

"Yay! Fireworks are most fun when you're with thousands of people in a parking lot. I probably won't miss the Clarks at all."

I buttered my pancake and poured syrup until Mom grabbed the bottle and said, "That's enough."

"Christa, don't be a drama queen," Amelia said. "I know it's the first year we've ever had friends here, and that it's the last year we'll ever see them, but family's more important."

"You're right," I said.

Dad sighed. Mom sighed. She looked at Dad and said, "I guess we didn't think this through."

"Rescheduling isn't easy," Dad said. "You see, girls, this coming weekend is our only three-day weekend until Labor Day. But maybe you both should be with your friends. We'll see those museums another time."

"I have an idea." Amelia sat up tall. "You guys used to have a date night like twice a month! You never do that anymore. Why don't you go to Duluth without us?"

"You've been teaching all summer," I said. "It's not fair you haven't done anything *you* want to do."

Dad's shoulders perked right up, but Mom's expression didn't change. "I'm not sure I want us to be apart on a holiday."

"Mom, you always think about us," Amelia said. "Maybe for one weekend you should think about you."

"What do you think?" Dad asked Mom. "The Clarks are right next door."

"Neil and Sally are leaving tomorrow for Arizona. Sally's sister had a baby. Alex is staying with Ed."

Dad nodded his head like it was settled. "So Ed will be here if the girls have any trouble."

Mom said, "Somehow I don't find that comforting." Then she squeezed Dad's hand. "I don't know, Todd. What do you think?"

"I think I'd love a date weekend with my wife." He leaned over and kissed her.

Dad smiled at Mom. Mom smiled at Dad. Amelia smiled at me. I smiled at everyone.

"All right, it's settled," Mom said. "But we need to tell you something. Remember the people who looked at the cabin with the new realtor? The ones who left because of what Alex said about bats? Well, Shawn explained everything. They really liked what they saw, so they're coming back to give it another look. Shawn thinks they'll buy it."

"AARRGGG!" Dad shrieked.

For a second I thought he was upset about the cabin, but then I saw the snake. It moved in an

S-shape from the bedroom door toward us. Then Mom saw it, too. She screamed, "AARRGGG!"

The snake glided across the floor, right toward me. I jumped up and stood on the kitchen chair, screaming, "AARRGGG!"

My parents scooted off their chairs and backed against the wall by the window.

"Get it, Todd!"

"Why do I have to get it? You're the science teacher. You get it."

"You saw it first!"

"Seeing it makes it my responsibility?"

Amelia swallowed the last of her orange juice while my parents argued. She tossed her hair to the side, stood up, and in one smooth move, picked up the snake. It wiggled in her hands. She grinned and lunged toward me. When I screamed, she laughed so hard I thought she might fall over and crush the snake, which would've been fine with me.

"Admit it. You're afraid of snakes."

"Am not! I'm just afraid of that one because it's a rare poisonous snake."

"It's a garter snake. It eats bugs and toads and mice." Amelia shoved it toward me again and laughed. "Who knew *you* were such a princess?"

"If it's poisonous and you die, it's your own fault," I said.

"Get that thing out of here!" Mom yelled.

"Okay, okay."

My heartbeat slowed as I watched Amelia push open the screen door with her hip and take the snake outside. I jumped off the chair and looked out the window. Amelia walked to the edge of the lawn and gently placed the snake on the ground. She watched it disappear into the brush.

My parents sat down and talked about how the snake could have possibly found its way into the cabin. They knew I wouldn't touch a snake, and they didn't seem to be considering Alex as a suspect.

I tuned out their words because I was stunned. Amelia My Sister had made a guest appearance. She'd snatched that snake like it was an adorable puppy. Maybe my sister, my real sister, was still under the shiny hair and lip gloss.

Then something in their conversation caught my ear. Dad was talking about Judy Garland's journals at the museum. How the journals would be a study of the times and a peek into her brain. How sad it was that journals now are typed into computers instead of handwritten, losing "the personality revealed in the style of the penmanship."

Dad said history-teacher stuff like that all the time, but this clanged in my ears.

Notebooks. Handwritten notebooks. A study of the times. A peek into the brain.

The notebook Alex had found in the basement wasn't just a bunch of recipes and weather reports. It had to be the journal of Mrs. Hillary Clark. Alex and I needed that notebook.

THE JOURNAL AND
THE DEAL

From that moment on, I behaved myself so nothing would make Mom and Dad cancel their trip to Duluth. I even thought about doing dishes, but I didn't want to make them suspicious. Amelia and I made a pact for peace, too. If we argued even once, our parents might decide we couldn't be trusted.

After work Friday, Mom and Dad stopped at the cabin to pack their bags and say goodbye.

"If you need anything at all, go talk to Ed," Dad told us.

"Or call my cell phone," Mom said. She quietly added, "We could drive here in the time it would take Ed to figure out something's wrong."

"It's fine, Mom," Amelia said.

"Remember, Amelia: no friends here. You can go to the party, but I don't want kids in the cabin while we're gone."

"I know!" Amelia said.

"And you . . ." Mom looked at me and sighed. "No trouble. I mean it."

"Zero trouble!"

Mom hugged us and Dad hugged us and then Mom hugged us again and then Dad hugged us again.

As soon as Mom and Dad were on their way to Duluth, Amelia went into our bedroom to watch a movie on her laptop. That was her definition of being in charge. Fine by me. Alex and I had a job to do.

Alex was outside washing the ATV. He wasn't allowed to ride it, but nobody said he couldn't touch

it or sit on it or wash it. Even though he had a
bucket of soapy water and a wet sponge, he was
covered in dirt.

"Hey, Alex! Are your parents gone?"

"They left this morning."

"Did you get the journal out of the basement?"

Alex shrugged, which told me the answer. I
couldn't believe it. Alex had one job to do. Just one:
get the journal out of the basement so we could
study it for clues.

"Grandpa said we're not supposed to go down
there, and I couldn't sneak around. It's like everyone was constantly watching."

"That's a complete load! You're chicken. You
know how important this is."

Before he could defend himself, Grumpa came
out of the house with a phone in his hand. He held
the phone at arm's length, like it might explode if
he carried it too close.

"Your parents decided we couldn't survive for
three days without a cellular phone. So your mom

left hers, and it's been beeping at me. There's a note on it that says 'missed call from Neil' and 'voice-mail.'"

"I'll show you how to listen to the message," Alex said.

"I've got a phone inside with a message machine. Why didn't your father just call that?"

"In case you weren't home. That's why. Let's just call him back. You just push this and this."

Grumpa shook his head like he'd never heard anything so dumb, but he held the phone against his cheek. "Neil, it's me . . . Uh huh . . . I don't think there's anything wrong with sugar before bedtime, but if you say so . . . Yes . . . Well, you have yourselves some fun out there." Grumpa shook his head again. "Hell's bells. He knows . . . Fine, fine." Grumpa pulled the phone from his face and said to Alex, "He says to tell you he loves you." Alex's face turned red and he rolled his eyes at me. Grumpa spoke into the phone again. "See, now you embarrassed him. Sons should know their fathers love them."

Just then it seemed Grumpa figured out a cell phone would let him talk *and* walk. He turned and went back to the house, mumbling into the phone.

Alex kneeled on the ground and started scrubbing the wheel.

"Are you kidding me, Alex? Who cares if the tires are clean?"

"I want it to sparkle."

"We have business. That journal isn't going to crawl out of the box and fly up the stairs. You said you'd take care of it. You said we could read it after my parents left."

"I didn't say—"

"Yes, you did! You said you'd take care of it."

"It's really dark down there at night. I didn't want to fall down the stairs and squish it."

I took the sponge from his hand and dropped it into the soapy bucket. "We're getting that journal."

We quietly went inside the house and tiptoed into the kitchen. The cell phone was on the kitchen table. We listened for signs that Grumpa was moving around the house.

"I don't hear anything," Alex whispered.

"I'll stand watch. You go get the journal."

"You go get it. I'm really good at watch-standing. Better than you."

"You're the one who found the journal. I don't know where it is. It's got to be you. If Grumpa comes into the kitchen, I'll cough. So just go."

Alex frowned.

"Fine." I pushed him away from the door. "I'll do it."

He pulled on my arm. He inhaled deep and long and said, "No. She's my great-grandmother. It's my basement. I'll go." Then he opened the door and disappeared into the basement.

I could hear the steps creaking as he made his way down. I worried Grumpa might come into the kitchen for a drink, but the house was quiet. I couldn't hear any movement in the basement, either. A few minutes later, the steps creaked until Alex stepped through the door.

"It's not there!" His eyes were huge. "Someone took it."

"Serious?"

"I wouldn't joke about this stuff."

"Did Mr. Walt Miller work in the basement?"

Alex smacked his forehead. "Yes! He came over last night while Grandpa was helping my mom with the accounting at the restaurant."

"You sure you looked in the right box?"

"Looking for this?" Grumpa had come from the living room, holding the old notebook above his head.

I'm not sure what was bigger—Alex's eyes or my fear that we were in trouble. Grumpa sat down at the kitchen table. He placed the notebook next to him, running his finger across it. "Take a seat."

Without a word we sat across from Grumpa. I stared at the table because I was afraid of his steel blue eyes. He was quiet for a minute.

"Ever since I retired, I can't stop thinking about it. My mother and Capone's money. All day. All night. I can't sleep. My head's about burning up."

Grumpa lifted his fishing hat and rubbed his head. "I read it after her funeral and put it in a box so I'd forget. And I didn't think about it for years. I worked and I had a family. When I lost my wife, I had to work even harder to keep everything out of my head. There was too much swirling around. Capone, my father, my mother, my wife."

Grumpa opened the notebook and paged through it. "She sure liked writing about the weather." He slid the notebook across the table to Alex. "Go ahead. Read this page."

Alex opened the notebook and blinked. "I don't read cursive very well."

"For the love of Gertrude, you don't know how to read?"

"I can read! But we didn't study frilly handwriting in my old school."

Grumpa was winding up for a big grump, I could tell. So I said, "My mom writes in cursive all the time."

"All right, Minnow, you read it."

I began:

My dearest Edmund,

I prayed and prayed for guidance after your father brought calamity to our home. I asked whether I should I spend this fortune on my son. I want a better life for you; however, I received no answer. I asked if I should donate it to people in need or if I should destroy it entirely. Still, I received no answers. Edmund, it pains me to confess my deception. I said I burned the money so you would not be consumed with the questions that have plagued me. Instead, I moved the fortune from one hiding place to another, until this morning.

Last night, I received an answer. I had a dream so real it was as though I lived it. In the dream, a voice told me to bury the money. When the building is lost, and the earth is moved again, the curse will lift.

In case someone finds this journal before my death, or before you read it, I will not disclose the location of the money. I left a note revealing the location in a place only you will know, my dear Edmund, a place from which it can escape.

When that day comes, Capone's fortune will rest in your hands. I pray you will find wisdom and strength to do what I could not.

Always your loving mother,
Hillary Clark

Grumpa's body looked heavy. I wondered what it felt like to hear a secret so old, a secret so heavy even a mother couldn't carry it.

Finally he spoke. "You probably won't understand, but the older you get, the more the past grabs you and shakes you and won't let go. I guess it's time to finish this once and for all."

I couldn't believe he put the notebook out of his mind for years and years. At what age did people decide there were things worth forgetting? I wanted to remember everything. "You read the journal, Grumpa, but you never looked for the other note?"

"That's right."

I read the line again. " 'I left a note revealing the location in a place only you will know, my dear

218

Edmund, a place from which it can escape.' That doesn't make sense. *A place from which it can escape.* What does that mean?"

"I know exactly what it means," Grumpa said. "Later tonight, after dark, I'm going to get that note."

"We'll go with you," Alex said.

"This is something I need to do by myself. I should've done it long ago. I want you kids to stay here. Amelia can keep an eye on you. I'll get you when I'm back."

"Why later?" I asked. "Why not now?"

"Because the restaurant doesn't close until ten," he said.

Alex and I passed time wading along the shore. The mosquitoes started their attack as soon as the sun dipped behind the trees. We went to the cabin for bug spray and found Amelia with company. Travis, Matt Sat-Flat, and another girl were sitting in our living room talking and laughing.

I wondered if the girl was with Matt and Travis when Sheriff Duncan chased them away from

Capone's hideout. If I hadn't been loaded in the back of a police car, I would have asked Sheriff Duncan to describe the teenagers he'd almost caught.

Amelia said, "Christa, this is Lara." I gave her a half smile while Amelia turned to her friends and announced, "Mr. Clark asked me to be in charge of the kids for a few hours. Think he's got a hot date?"

Over their laughter I said, "You're not supposed to have friends visit when Mom and Dad aren't here."

"It's not a big deal. We're just hanging out and watching movies."

"Still, you're not supposed to."

"Guess what else is not supposed to happen?" Amelia let that question hang in the air before she pounced. "You're not supposed to be busted by a cop for riding an ATV out to Capone's hideout!"

My mouth dropped open. "Did Grumpa say something?"

"So old Ed Clark has kids doing his dirty work." Travis smiled as though he'd solved a mystery.

Alex's eyes looked like bullets. "My grandpa told

us to stop digging around. He said he's going to take care of it himself."

"Is that why Amelia is babysitting?" Matt asked. "So he can run around Capone's woods in the dark?"

"He's not running around. He . . . he . . . he has to help with the accounting at the restaurant," Alex said.

"Amelia, do Mom and Dad know about the ATV?" I asked.

Amelia let me wonder and worry. She smiled while my heart raced. Her friends laughed. Finally, she said, "Mom and Dad don't know. I know because Matt told me. Walt Miller is Matt's grandfather."

Just then the puzzle came together. Alex's expression told me he got it, too. Mr. Walt Miller and Matt Ratty Rat-Rat were big mouths *and* relatives, and they were working together to steal the money. Matt probably didn't even like Amelia. He was using her to get closer to the Clarks!

"How about a deal, Christa? I'll won't tell Mom

and Dad about the ATV if you don't say anything about my friends being here."

Amelia didn't understand what was really happening, and this was no time to tell her. "Fine. We're going to Alex's since you'll be hogging the TV."

"Just don't get arrested." Amelia's little joke made her friends laugh and laugh.

FINDING AND
KEEPING

Alex and I drank orange soda and ate leftover pizza while we waited for Grumpa. The Clarks' refrigerator held boxes of leftover pizza every single night. Alex was so lucky.

The phone rang, and we both jumped. It was the loudest ring I'd ever heard. Grumpa's phone was an artifact. It hung on the wall, and a corkscrew-shaped cord connected its parts. Alex answered, muttered a few words about Grumpa not being home, that he was helping with business stuff at the restaurant, and then hung up.

"Weird," he said. "That was Walt Miller. He wanted to talk to Grandpa. He said he wanted to know if Grandpa was feeling better."

I jumped up. "He's lying, Alex. I bet anything Matt called his grandfather right after we left the cabin. Mr. Walt Miller thinks Grumpa is going to get Capone's loot."

"And now he's off to catch him," Alex finished.

"Why'd you open your big mouth and say Grumpa was helping your parents with the accounting? Now Mr. Walt Miller knows he went to the restaurant!"

I expected an Alex shrug, but he marched to the door and put on his shoes. "We've got to get to Grandpa before he does. Hurry up."

We rumbled into town on the ATV. Alex parked in the alley behind the restaurant where the light was dim. He followed me through the entrance, which was unlocked. Grumpa obviously had no idea his buddy was a crook.

I'd never seen the restaurant dark and quiet. The napkin dispensers were placed in the middle of every table with a jar of Parmesan cheese on one side and red peppers on the other. The chairs were tucked perfectly under red-and-white tablecloths. Even without the ovens running, there were delicious smells in the air—dough and sausage and garlic bread.

Light shined from the crack between the floor and the basement door. Slowly I opened the door. Alex went first, and I followed. Grumpa stood by the big freezer, messing with its lock.

Grumpa's head didn't move. He said, "This lock is awful rusty. I don't want to force it and snap the key." He adjusted his fishing hat and looked at us. "Took you longer to get here than I expected."

"Are you mad?" Alex asked.

"Would it make a difference?"

"Sorry," Alex said, "but we needed to get here before Walt Miller."

Grumpa wiggled the key again. "Walt? I've known that guy my whole life, and I can tell you exactly where he is right now. Sleeping."

"He's after the money," I told him. "Sheriff

Duncan almost caught his grandson Matt at Capone's hideout."

Grumpa stopped and squinted. "Now how would you know that?"

"The sheriff told us," I said.

"He said Matt Miller trespassed out at Capone's?"

"Not exactly," Alex said. "He said he'd chased off some teenagers, and we figured it had to be Matt and his buddies. They've snooped down here, too. Matt told Christa's family he'd poked around the basement."

"Half the people in town have poked around this basement," Grumpa said. "Even Duncan's been down here. Before he was a sheriff, he was a pesky teen just like the others. I caught him myself years ago with one of the cooks."

"You need better locks," I said.

Grumpa let out an old-man chuckle-cough. "My mother outsmarted Capone's professional goons. I figure I can outsmart a bunch of kids."

"Let me help," Alex said.

"I got it." He jiggled the lock. "You're a fine helper, Alex. You should've been helping me for the last eleven years. I should've fixed up things with Neil long ago. I was a stubborn fool."

The door popped off, and a blast of stink hit us. The freezer didn't smell like rotting food, though, more like old sneakers and stale water. Grumpa turned on a flashlight and waved a beam of light inside. The freezer was about the size of two bathrooms. Boxes and junk leaned against its walls.

Alex stepped inside. "What's all the stuff?"

"My mother believed nothing should be wasted. Everything had a second or third use." Grumpa inspected the contents with his flashlight. "Jugs and fry pans. Some kerosene lamps." He peeked inside a box. "And look here. Leather-bound menus."

I took a menu from the box and ran my fingers over the cracked leather. Gold letters formed the words "Clarks Fine Dining." This menu could've been in the hands of Al Capone! Maybe Capone smudged steak grease on it. Maybe the menu sat next to his plate while he talked about hiding his fortune from the cops. This menu was part of Mrs. Hillary Clark and the pro-booze people and the anti-booze people and Capone and all his goons. It was a real part of a real story. I understood why my dad loved artifacts.

"What exactly are we looking for?" Alex asked.

"The first half of the clue was this freezer. So now we have to figure out where she put the note. It's got to be in here somewhere."

Alex repeated the clue: "'I left a note revealing the location in a place only you will know, my dear Edmund, a place from which it can escape.' I don't get it, Grandpa."

"Just start looking."

"Should we be looking for something that you'd have to escape from? Like locks or ropes or chains?" I asked.

"Look for another notebook. Or just a note. It's got to be in here." Grumpa paused, closed his eyes, and rubbed his head.

"Are you okay?" I asked.

He almost smiled—almost. "I am. I'm down-right good, as a matter of fact, like I'm finally swatting a fly that's been pestering me since I was a kid."

We looked through boxes with the flashlight. The boxes held loads of old kitchen supplies—cheese jars, coffee cups, mugs, fancy napkins. I wanted to examine everything I picked up, but there wasn't time. As Grumpa bent down to look through another box, I noticed a taxidermied bird high on a freezer shelf.

"Grumpa, can you reach that?"

He snagged the bird with a big stretch. Just like the mounted animals near Grumpa's worktable, the bird had an engraved plate that said *For My Edmund*.

"All the other ones your mom made are at the house," Alex said. "Why is there only one here?"

Grumpa inspected it. He gently pulled and twisted the bird, but it stayed firmly on the mount. He tapped on the base and squeezed the bird's head.

He picked at the *For My Edmund* plate, but it didn't budge. Finally he twisted the wood base, hard, separating it from the bird.

The top of the base opened and inside the wood was a carved hole with a piece of paper.

"Read it!" I practically jumped up and down.

He gave Alex the flashlight to shine on the paper. "It says, 'Dearest Edmund, the suitcase is hidden next to our house. I buried it in the spot Gerald Westman marked for the cabin he is building.'"

It didn't make sense right away. Grumpa said, "Hell's bells! She buried it when Gerald Westman started digging to build the cabin. Your cabin, Minnow. You've been sleeping on loot your whole life."

A voice deep and low, from behind a bright flashlight, said, "Good to know. I never would've thought to look there."

Sheriff Duncan.

Grumpa nearly dropped the flashlight. Alex and I pressed our backs against the boxes while Grumpa muttered, "Duncan? Nobody called you for help. This ain't your business."

"Who said I'm here to help?" I didn't understand what Sheriff Duncan meant until he said, "It's easy to break into places when you've got a badge. See, I've been looking for that money for nearly thirty years, old man. I've been in Capone's hideout and every building he ever set foot inside. I've been down here at least half a dozen times."

"You're supposed to be the law!" Grumpa's face looked fierce.

"So your mother buried it underneath that cabin by your house. That's not very convenient, is it?"

"That's my cabin," I yelled.

The sheriff tapped the gun in his belt with his knuckle. I shut up. He said, "Give me the freezer key, Ed."

"Bad men make bad money, Duncan."

"I'll take my chances. Don't make me pull my gun. Just give me the key."

Grumpa's hand shook as he handed the key to Duncan. Grumpa backed up, so we did, too.

"You can't lock us in here!" Alex shouted.

"Go ahead and yell. Nobody will hear you." The door slammed shut, and the lock clicked. Footsteps pounded up the stairs, and then there was nothing except the sound of us breathing.

DIRT AND
MORE DIRT

Alex pounded on the sides of the freezer while I kicked the door. He yelled, "Open up, Duncan!"

Duncan. He didn't deserve to be called Sheriff Duncan or Mr. Sheriff Duncan. He was worse than Al Capone, worse than all of Capone's thugs combined. Capone never pretended to be a good guy. He was bad and everyone knew it.

"Open up!"

Grumpa grabbed Alex's arm. "Stop. Duncan's right. Nobody can hear you."

"When the restaurant opens tomorrow, how

long will it be before someone comes down here?" My voice didn't hide fear. "Does someone come down here three times a day? Twice a day? Once?" Grumpa was quiet, and I couldn't see his face. "How often? Answer me!"

"Nobody's supposed to come down here, period," Grumpa said. "But we've got a way out. The clue said the note is in 'a place from which it *can* escape.' That place is right here, right in this freezer."

"I don't get it," I said.

"When this basement was a bar, we needed an escape route. When the cops came, customers would get into this freezer. The panel at the end is a fake. They'd open it up and escape through the back."

"Escape to where?" Alex asked.

"The tunnel." Grumpa handed Alex the flashlight. He pushed and pulled on the back panel until it popped off. Behind it, a hole in the wall led to a dirt tunnel. The tunnel was just a few inches higher than Grumpa and probably three feet wide.

Dust drifted into the freezer. My eyes burned.

Grumpa stepped into the tunnel and waved for us to follow. "I hope it hasn't caved in."

We stuck close to Grumpa as he scanned the tunnel with the flashlight. I'd never seen such darkness. The tunnel swallowed the beam of light. I was afraid it would swallow us, too, trapping us with no light and no air.

Grumpa said, "This tunnel goes under the street. It's not long."

Untouched for decades, the space seemed to come alive as we moved through it. Dirt came down in a fine mist, and spiders scurried from the light. Grumpa jumped as a furry mass darted in front of us. Alex backed into me, knocking me against the dirt wall. A chunk of mud dropped and landed on my foot.

"Just a mole," Grumpa said.

I'd never seen a mole before, but I knew from Amelia that moles had tiny eyes buried in coarse fur. She said their heads looked like eyeless blobs with snouts and spiked teeth. I shuddered, thinking about moles wriggling around my feet, sniffing with long snouts. Moles. Moles and snakes. The tunnel might be full of them, and if the flashlight gave out, we'd be blind. We'd be able to hear them scurry and hiss, and feel them brush against our ankles, but our eyes would fail us. We wouldn't know what to kick or where to run.

I wished we were pretend trapped in a pit that was really Grumpa's basement and pretend chased by zanimals that were really Grumpa's taxidermy.

I tugged Grumpa's shirt. "Will you give me a piggyback?"

"Just keep moving," Grumpa whispered. "Slow but steady."

The flashlight teased with flickers of things— a stick, an old shoe, a broken bottle, a man's hat. Every few feet I could make out wood beams supporting the tunnel's walls and ceiling. I wanted to touch the wood and feel something sturdy, something that couldn't collapse, but I was afraid the wood had rotted into mush. One hand, one elbow, might bring the beams down.

The ground was uneven, and my shoes squeezed

into the earth. I lost my balance and landed on my knees in the damp earth. The fall made me cough, and dirt trickled down. I scrambled to my feet, thinking about moles and snakes.

"You okay?" Alex asked.

"Totally."

"Take it slow," Grumpa whispered. He held my arm at the elbow and pulled me along.

"I'm scared." Alex's voice shook. "I wanna go back!"

Grumpa let go of my elbow and patted Alex's shoulder. "Remember what I told you about staying calm? Think about being somewhere else. Tell yourself it's not dark; it's not dirty; you're not scared."

The flashlight showed Alex nodding and wiping his face. Grumpa turned and led us deeper into the tunnel. Finally he stopped. Finally.

We'd come to a brick wall with a hole covered from the other side by a wood board. Grumpa handed the flashlight to Alex and pushed on the wood. The slab didn't move, but dirt rained down from overhead. Grumpa pushed harder as ground dropped around us.

"Hell's bells!"

Alex yelled, "Grandpa! We're going to be buried!"

Coughing rattled my body. I brushed the dirt off my head, but it kept coming. Grumpa backed up and threw his entire weight at the board. He rubbed his shoulder while Alex tried kicking it loose.

"It's not moving," Alex said.

Even though I was coughing, I threw my weight against the board, too.

"Stand back!"

Grumpa slammed against the board again and again until I heard a *crack*. The board split open. As he gave it a final push, I leaned to my right—just a bit—and my elbow pierced the side of the tunnel. Dirt poured down my leg and piled wet and cold around my ankle. I could feel grit in my shoes.

With a tug on my arm, Grumpa pulled me through the hole, and the three of us were standing in a cramped space. I reached out and felt a solid wall around me. We coughed and gasped and brushed dirt off our bodies. It looked like we were in a concrete closet with the hole behind us and a grate the size of a door in front of us.

"Where are we?" I asked.

When Grumpa had caught his breath, he said, "Pops needed to get supplies and booze and people in and out this way. So the tunnel was connected to the building people least suspected. The library."

The grate gave way with a kick, and we stepped inside a larger stone room. We could barely move because the space was crammed with a huge metal drum with pipes attached to it. "That's the old boiler. It's how they used to heat the building."

In the front of the boiler was yet another door. It opened easily, and we stepped into a basement, an old and damp basement like the one in Clarks Pizza. I couldn't stop coughing. Alex sneezed and rubbed his eyes. With a wave of the flashlight, Grumpa pointed to a switch on the wall. I raced across the room and turned on the ceiling light.

Grumpa didn't look right. His eyes were red

from the dust and dirt. His breaths came hard, and he stumbled across the floor and steadied himself once he reached the wall.

"Grandpa! Are you okay?"

"Think I busted my ribs taking down that door. But we're in the library now. Just give me a second to catch my breath."

Alex took Grumpa's hand and led him around a corner to a storage area. Packed into the room were a copy machine, boxes of paper, shelves with office supplies, and several old computers. A few feet from the shelves was a staircase.

Grumpa leaned against the wall and slid down until he was sitting on the floor. Alex kneeled next to him. Grumpa said, "Here's what's going to happen. You two are going to get on that ATV and go to the cabin." He paused, struggling to get a breath. "Get Amelia and those kids out of there. No packing, no talking. Don't call the police. Duncan may not be working alone and besides, he'd hear on his radio. When you're far away, have Amelia call Walt Miller. He'll know what to do."

I said, "We'll come back here first to get you and take you with us."

"Did I say anything about you coming back here? No, I didn't."

Grumpa rumbled Alex's hair and said, "Don't crash that ATV. I hate it when your dad's right and I'm wrong."

"You're going to be all right." Alex patted Grumpa's shoulder.

"Hell's bells. Course I am."

"No, I mean it."

"I mean it, too."

"I really mean it, Grandpa. You're going to be all right." Alex squeezed Grumpa's shoulder. "You will. I know you will. Right?"

Grumpa rested his head against the wall. "I'm already better."

Alex patted his shoulder again. Then he stood up, rushed past me, and darted up the stairs. I turned to follow him when I heard Grumpa say, "Minnow! Come here."

I shuffled back and kneeled next to him.

Grumpa's face was gray under the dirt. I grabbed his hand and squeezed it. He didn't squeeze back.

"What?"

"Let it rest. Okay? Let it rest."

"Grumpa, are you really okay?"

"That's enough. Go."

I went.

THE CHASE AND
THE ESCAPE

The ATV blasted down the county road with
Alex in front and me behind him hanging on tight.
We rumbled to a stop at the intersection before his
house. He turned off the engine and took off his
helmet.

"Alex! Are you crazy? Get moving!"

"The ATV is too loud. If Duncan's there, he'll
hear us. Help me hide it. Let's get it as far in the
brush as we can."

"Good idea." We each grabbed a handle bar and
pushed the ATV down the ditch, through the

weeds, and into the brush. Then we ran toward the cabin and his house.

We were nearly to his driveway when he grabbed my arm. "Wait. Let's check it out and make sure he's not already here."

"Okay."

Another good idea. As we crouched behind a pine tree, I realized Alex's brain was moving faster than mine. I needed to catch up, and the catching up wasn't about a race to be the best. Not this time. I thought about Grumpa in the library, not able to help us, and Amelia in the cabin, not knowing that she needed help. We wouldn't beat Duncan without two brains working together.

"Everything looks okay," I said. "Let's make a run for it."

We ran to the cabin door. Amelia and her friends were in the same spots as when we left them, only now a movie was playing. Amelia pressed the pause button.

"We've got to get out of here!" I said.

"You're covered in dirt," Amelia said. "What—"

"Never mind that!" I yelled. "Listen. The sheriff locked us in the freezer at the restaurant and we got stuck in an underground tunnel and broke into the library and now Grumpa's there and Duncan is coming here to steal the money that's buried here."

Amelia, Matt, Travis, and Lara all looked at each other, then at us. Everyone burst out laughing—everyone except Matt. I turned off the TV. "Grumpa says we have to leave now and call Mr. Walt Miller because he'll know what to do."

Amelia was still laughing when Matt grabbed her arm and said, "I don't think she's kidding."

"We're not kidding!" Alex yelled.

"My grandpa's always said the sheriff shouldn't have a badge, that he's a bad guy," Matt said.

Amelia asked, "Why would he think that?"

"Years ago, Grandpa saw him sneaking out the back of the Rod 'n' Reel Bar late at night. The next day he heard the bar had been broken into and money was stolen. Mr. Clark told Grandpa to forget about reporting it because nobody would believe him, and Duncan would start following

Grandpa around, giving him tickets for every little thing. My grandpa says Duncan doesn't deserve a badge."

Nobody was laughing anymore. Amelia took a breath. "This is all really weird. Can we just start from the beginning?"

Before I could speak, Alex said, "We'll tell you all about it in the car, but we have to get out of here. Capone's loot is buried underneath this cabin. Duncan's coming to get it."

"Here?" Amelia said. "There's money *here*?"

We all heard it at once—the sound of a car coming up the driveway. Travis peeked through the blinds. "It's a police car!"

"Oh my God!" Amelia gasped. "What are we going to say?"

"Just stay quiet!" Matt said.

A car door opened and shut. I'd never noticed the sound of breathing until that moment. My breath seemed even louder than my heartbeat, and my heartbeat could've been a drum.

There was a knock at the door.

Matt held his finger against his lips.

Another knock—this one louder.

Alex mouthed a question to me: "Is the door locked?"

It wasn't.

"Anyone there?" Duncan called from outside.

I leaped toward the door, thinking I could quickly and quietly turn the lock, but I was too slow. Duncan opened the door. I froze, but so did he. The sheriff's eyes snapped back and forth from me to Alex.

"How'd you get here?" His voice rumbled.

In a blur, Matt jumped in front of me, slammed the door, and turned the lock. Duncan banged on the door. "Don't listen to those two. They're full of lies! Open up!"

"You're the liar," Alex yelled. "Just wait 'til everyone finds out what you did!"

The sheriff's voice got fast and higher pitched. "Let's talk about this. Matt Miller, I know you're in there. Listen to me. Those kids are up to no good. Open the door and I'll explain everything."

Lara whispered, "Let's call 9-1-1."

"Are you kidding?" Travis said. "The call will go to him."

Duncan pounded harder. "You want trouble? Because you'll get it!"

"What are we going to do?" Amelia asked.

"I will kick this door down!" Duncan yelled.

My brain kicked into gear. "We can crawl out the window in Mom and Dad's bedroom. It's the only way."

Everyone followed me into my parents' room. Matt popped off the screen, and one by one he boosted us up and out. He jumped down to the ground and said, "Duncan's kicking at the door. Now what?"

Lara grabbed Matt's arm. "If the money is under the cabin, how's he going to get it?"

"We don't have time to think about that," Travis said. "We've got to get out of here."

Amelia patted her back pocket. "I've got my car keys and my phone."

"We can't go to the driveway. He'll see us," I said.

"Okay," Amelia said. "So we'll make a run for the woods. There might be a boat docked at the landing. If not, we'll run to the cabins toward the east side of the lake."

From inside the cabin it sounded like the door was breaking open. Matt looked in the window. "He's inside. Run!"

We ran across the yard and into the waist-high weeds leading to the woods. The weeds scratched our legs and tangled around our feet, but we moved quickly into the cover of trees. We stopped and huddled together.

Duncan's voice cut through the night. "If you come out now, I won't even give you a ticket."

"Don't answer," Amelia whispered. "He might give up and go away."

"Those little kids are confused. Whatever they told you, they got it wrong." I couldn't hear his movement over the song of crickets and frogs, but his voice sounded closer. Amelia squeezed my shoulder. I leaned into her and inhaled. Her weird body spray filled me up, and I felt calm for a few seconds.

Then his words came faster. "You want to end up in juvenile court? Your parents will be madder than hell. You'll ruin your chance for college. You'll . . . have a record . . . and you won't be able to get jobs. You'll be poor. And jail! You'll go to jail! I can make that happen. I can. You don't want that."

"He's not making any sense," Matt said.

"He knows he's been caught, and he's not backing down," Amelia said. "Come on, let's go. There's almost always a boat at the landing. If there aren't keys, we'll use the emergency oars. Once we're on the lake he won't be able to get us."

We started running again. The weeds rustled as creatures scattered and ran from us. My heart pounded faster than my footsteps. What if there wasn't a boat at the landing? What if there was a boat, but it was just a two-person canoe?

"Stop! I mean it!" Duncan's voice was getting closer.

The night grew darker as the trees thickened. Branches slapped against my face, and my ankles burned from thistle. I heard an "oomph!" from Lara as she slammed into a tree.

"I think my nose is bleeding," she cried.

"Get behind me in a line," Amelia said. She held out her arms, feeling in front of her, and guided us carefully but quickly through brush and branches. "Hurry!"

Duncan yelled, "I've got a Taser and I'll use it!"

I wondered how close he'd have to be for a Taser to shock us. He was catching up while we seemed to be slowing down. The ground was clogged with brush. The weeds scratched my legs from my ankles to the bottom of my shorts.

Finally the trees spread apart and became open ground. We reached the blacktop driveway where people put boats into the lake. Westman's boat landing.

The dock was empty. No boat. No canoe. Not even an inner tube.

"Now what?" Alex asked.

The trees rustled behind us.

"Now what?" Alex repeated.

There were two places to go: the road, where we'd be in the open, or the water, which was cloaked in darkness. Duncan didn't give us a choice. He popped out of the trees and stood between us and the road.

Amelia yelled, "Get in the lake! We'll . . . we'll swim somewhere."

We plunged into the water. I'd never been in the lake at night. The water was dark and terrible, as dark and terrible as the tunnel, nothing like its gentle ripple on a hot afternoon. Cold shot from my ankles to my waist to my chest.

"Swim out 'til he can't see us," Amelia said.

Duncan called to us, "Don't be stupid! It doesn't have to be like this."

"Alex can't swim!" I splashed until I had Alex's arm.

Matt glided between us. "Kick off your shoes. They'll weigh you down."

Alex gasped. "I can't go any deeper. I can't reach."

"We've got to get farther away." Matt tugged at Alex. "I don't know what will happen if he shocks us with that Taser while we're in the water."

Travis asked, "How far out?"

"I don't know," Matt said. "He's got a gun, too. Just keep going."

Duncan waved his flashlight at us. "Fine, fine. What happens now is *your* fault. There's nowhere for you to go. You can't make it across the lake, and you can't tread water for long. You might as well come back. I've got all the time in the world."

Alex yelled, "You could've killed us in that freezer! We could have suffocated!"

"You should've stayed out of the way! I've been after that money since I was a kid. You think you can just wander into my town and look for my money?"

"You're going to jail!" Alex's head bobbed, making him swallow and spit up water. Matt tried to calm him while Duncan laughed and said, "Sorry, kid. You're wrong."

Alex's head bobbed again. I started to tread

water because I could no longer touch bottom. "I'll help you, Alex. Hang on to my shoulders." My voice shook because I didn't really know how to help him. I didn't know if I could swim for both of us. My parents never let me swim in the lake without a life jacket.

"No, Christa. He'll drag you underwater," Matt said. "Alex, hold my shoulders. Not so tight! Better. Okay, kick with me."

My body was heavy. I put my right foot against the shoe on my left heel and pushed the shoe off. I did the same to my right shoe. Matt was right. I felt lighter.

We swam into deeper water.

"I can keep you pinned down until you can't swim anymore," Duncan called from behind the beam of his flashlight.

"And how are you going to explain that?" Matt said. "You can't. You're not thinking straight! Get out of here while you can, Duncan!"

"Get out of that water while *you* can!"

Travis's voice came from yards away. I couldn't

even see him. "There's six of us and one of you. Who do you think people will believe?"

"It's easy to explain. A group of careless teenagers leave on the gas oven and take off for a joyride. They steal a boat and speed around the lake at night. No light on the boat. No life jackets. No common sense. The cabin burns down, and the kids have a boating accident and drown. A tragedy."

Lara shouted, "That's insane! Nobody will believe you."

"You mean the police won't believe me?" Duncan yelled back. "Kids, I am the police!"

My arms and legs felt heavy. Alex gulped and coughed water. Matt grunted as he tried to swim with Alex clinging to his back.

"Is Alex okay?" I swam closer to Matt and Alex.

Alex said, "I can float. I don't need to swim."

"Good idea, buddy." Matt's words came between strained breaths. "Get on your back and let go of me. I'll stay right here."

"You okay, Matt?" Travis yelled.

"Nothing like a refreshing nighttime swim!" Matt's voice was not as lighthearted as his words.

My arms moved in the shape of an eight, treading water to keep me afloat. I felt cold from my neck to my toes, and I was getting tired. I wondered what my parents would think if Duncan's plan worked. Would they believe him because I was immature? Would they think I'm the type of kid who'd forget a hot oven and let a cabin catch fire? They'd never believe Amelia could be so careless.

Then my heart about stopped. "Where's Amelia? Amelia? Where is she?"

I was close enough to see Matt's eyes go wide. Matt, Travis, and Lara started to call for her. Amelia hadn't been swimming in the lake for two years. She wasn't strong anymore. She wasn't used to the cold gripping her muscles. Whitefish Lake was deep—more than one hundred feet in some spots. The lake warmed slightly in the summer heat, but the deep spots were cold. Already my hands were numb.

Matt grabbed my arm and pulled me closer to him and Alex. "Okay, Alex, you're floating. Don't stop floating. I've got to find her."

Matt swam toward Lara and Travis. Their voices seemed to float into the sky and fade in the darkness.

Alex's teeth chattered.

"You'll stay warmer if you move instead of float," I gasped.

"I'm okay. I have to be okay because Grandpa will want to see me later. Just like Amelia will want to see you later."

"Amelia should be answering them by now!"

Duncan's voice broke through the calls for Amelia. "One kid down, five to go!"

"I hate you! I—" My screams stopped with a mouthful of water.

"Pretend Duncan isn't here," Alex said. "I'm not letting myself hear him. I'm not letting myself think about the water." I felt his hand on mine. "Christa, look at the stars."

"I'm so cold."

"It's not c-c-c-cold at all!" Alex shivered. "It's like the sun is pounding on us."

"I'm so tired."

"Float with me and look at the stars." Alex pulled on my arm. "Don't listen to anything. Just look at the s-s-s-stars. Look straight up. The stars make the shape of a Christmas tree. See it?"

I gulped water and coughed.

"Christa, float. Just lean back and look up."

I pressed back into the water and floated, squeezing Alex's hand. I could hear Lara, Travis, and Matt splashing around, yelling Amelia's name, but they seemed far away.

"Do you see it, Christa? Do you s-s-s-see the Christmas tree?"

I whispered, "I don't see a tree. I see a bow and arrow."

"I see a cat's face and whiskers."

"I see a birthday cake."

"I'm not c-c-cold," he said through shivers. "Not at all."

"Me neither."

"Do you see the hand and the flame from the Statue of Liberty?"

"Where's my s-s-s-sister, Alex?"

"Just keep looking," he said. "I see . . . lights. I see lights."

"I see—"

"No, I mean I see lights!" His hand jerked away from me, and he pointed to the boat landing. A beam of light turned from the road onto Westman's landing. A car. Duncan's shape turned into a silhouette in the headlights.

The engine roared. Tires squealed. The car lurched forward. In a blink, the car smashed into the sheriff and sent him airborne. He rolled over the windshield and landed in a heap in the weeds. The car stopped with the front wheels just short of the lake.

The door opened, and Amelia stepped out. Amelia My Sister.

FANTASTIC AND
JUST LIKE THAT

After Amelia knocked out Sheriff Duncan, Matt ran through the trees to the Clarks' house and called his grandfather, Mr. Walt Miller, who sent police officers from the next town. They carted Duncan away in an ambulance.

Amelia told us how she'd swum toward the cabin, crawled to the shore when she was out of sight, and ran like a bullet to get the car. Her phone was dead, but the keys were still tucked in her back pocket.

Mom and Dad drove back from Duluth while Neil and Sally got on a plane in Arizona.

After Mr. Walt Miller called the cops from the next town, he raced to Hayward and broke into the library with an ax to save Grumpa. The ambulance took Grumpa to the emergency room, and doctors there transferred him to the big hospital in Duluth.

Alex and his parents got to see Grumpa the next day. Alex told me Neil patted Grumpa on the shoulder and said he was a heck of a fighter, and Grumpa actually laughed and fake-boxed with Alex.

So everything turned out. We did not suffocate in a freezer or get buried in a tunnel. We didn't crash the ATV on the highway or drown in the lake. Grumpa did not die in the library basement. The fact that we knew where Al Capone's long-lost loot was buried was like having dessert after dessert.

Then everything turned upside down.

Grumpa died in the middle of the night.

When I went to bed, he was alive. When I woke up, he was dead.

Just like that.

LOUD WORDS
AND PICKLES

Amelia and I were getting dressed for the funeral when we heard our parents talking in the kitchen. Amelia zipped up my dress, which Mom had had to buy in town. We didn't have funeral clothes at the cabin.

Suddenly my parents' words got loud.

"I'm not prepared to make a decision, Todd!"

"We've made our decision. This doesn't change anything."

"There's money under our cabin. Isn't that a game changer?"

My dad's answer was soft, and then I couldn't hear them at all.

Shawn Weller's buyers had made an offer on our cabin, and they wanted an answer in forty-eight hours. My parents didn't know what to do. Amelia didn't know what to do. But I knew what to do. I knew because Grumpa had told me to *let it rest*.

I didn't tell my parents about Grumpa's words. I couldn't tell them because whenever I thought about Grumpa in the library—even for a second—I felt dizzy and sweaty. The air left my lungs and couldn't get back in. I figured my parents would decide to *let it rest*, that they'd sell the cabin without my saying a word. And that was okay with me. Without Grumpa, the cabin was just a bunch of old boards and rusty nails.

Amelia handed me her hairbrush, which I nearly dropped because Dad started yelling, "Ed Clark isn't even in the ground, and you want to talk about money? Unbelievable!"

"No, I don't. I want to go to a funeral and cry,

like a normal human being, but the clock is ticking."

Amelia flopped on her bunk and groaned, "I can't believe this is happening."

Maybe I was wrong about my parents. Apparently Mom believed in finders keepers. Who knew? I opened the bedroom door with a bang, and they immediately turned on their smiles. Mom hugged and kissed me and then wrapped her arms around Amelia. We'd been hugged and kissed so much in the past few days I felt squished.

Mom picked up her purse and walked past my dad without looking at him. "Let's go, girls."

Grumpa's funeral overflowed with people. The cooks and servers from Clarks Pizza were there. Mr. Walt Miller and Matt sat with their family. Nan was there. So was the guy who ran the ice cream shop and the man who took tickets at the National Fresh Water Fishing Hall of Fame. Even the fudge lady was there.

From our pew, I could see Alex walk with his parents from the church office to the front pew.

Neil's face was wet from crying. I couldn't stand to look at Neil, not when he seemed so sad, so I studied Alex. His face was actually clean, and his hair was slicked back. He wore a black suit that seemed to swallow him. His mom had gone shopping, too.

Everything about the funeral was wrong. The Clarks should have dressed Grumpa in his fishing hat instead of a brown suit, and the pastor should've said "Hell's bells" instead of reading from the Bible. Even the smells were wrong. I nearly coughed from all the old lady perfume. It mixed with Amelia's body spray and made me gag. Grumpa would have wanted the church to smell like dough or fish or even fish guts.

Just thinking about what Grumpa would've wanted at his funeral led my mind to the last thing he'd wanted. *Let it rest.*

The very words made my chest ache. I couldn't look at my parents because they were crying, and I couldn't look at the pastor because he stood next to the casket that held Grumpa. It seemed the weight of it all would crush me. The air was leaving my lungs, and I felt like I might fall out of the pew.

I couldn't take it a second longer. I wondered what Chase Truegood would do at Grandfather Punch's funeral, but the funeral was too awful for play thinking. Still, I needed to get away from those thoughts. When I was at school, and math made me feel like I might explode, I moved around until the feeling went away.

So I started swinging my legs fast and hard. Dad nudged me, so instead of leg swinging I picked up the songbook and tried to balance it on the very tip of my knee. The book held steady for a few seconds, then dropped with a thud. Dad snatched it off the floor.

My lungs filled up, and the pain behind my eyes faded. It was working.

Mom had given me tissues in case I got the eye sweats, so I took one and tore it into strips. I tied strips from the tissue around my fingers, like little rings, until Mom grabbed the whole wad and shoved it in her purse.

Then I made a tent with my skirt. I slipped my shoes off and on and off and on. While everyone sang, I rolled my tongue, stuck it through my lips, and blew air, making the tiniest hint of a whistle. I wondered if there was a dog nearby who could hear it.

Suddenly the funeral was over and we were going into the basement for a funeral lunch.

It'd worked so well, I decided to keep making it work.

A long table near the kitchen was covered with food: ham sandwiches, baked beans, pickles, cheese slices, nuts, carrots, and Jell-O salad, which is the only salad I like. Alex was already sitting at a table with his parents and Mr. Walt Miller. He saw me and gave a small wave. I small-waved back.

I loaded up my plate with pickles—pickles and pickles and pickles until Dad grabbed my hand and said, "That's enough." I stacked cheese slices about an inch high, but the line stopped. People waited while servers refilled the sandwich plate. All the waiting made me think about *let it rest*, and

I didn't want to picture Grumpa on the library floor. I didn't want to stand there waiting and thinking.

Thankfully, the boy in front of me was Quincy. I poked his back. "Hi, Quincy."

He frowned at me. Since his parents and little sister were right next to him, he couldn't say anything mean. He mumbled, "Hello."

Quincy turned away, so I poked him again. "You're not even wearing a suit."

"So?"

"So? It's a funeral. You shouldn't be wearing tan pants."

Dad nudged me. Then he smiled at Quincy. "You look very nice."

Quincy's little sister crammed between us. She stared up at me, smiled all big, and said, "Your dress is pretty." Then she put her finger in her nose and started to pick.

"Gross!"

Quincy's mom grabbed her hand while Quincy rolled his eyes. "She does that all the time." He told me, "She picked her nose when she was on Santa's lap."

"That's nothing," I said. "My sister ran over a cop."

Dad grabbed my plate out of my hands, left it on the serving table, and pulled me by my arm into the tiny hall.

"Stop it immediately! You're acting like a toddler, and I'm absolutely ashamed!"

In a half second, my face was wet with tears, not eye sweats, but tears that gushed. It was the kind of crying where even noise can't escape. Dad took me to the corner of the hall, by the bathroom marked *Men*. He put his arms around me, and we stayed there until I was cried out.

MAYBE AND
MAYBE NOT

My parents still had to make a decision about Shawn Weller's buyers, quickly.

For a few hours, it seemed like Dad had won. He said if money had been buried in a 1930s suitcase, or even a solid wood box, it would have rotted. That money would've been worm food shortly after it was buried. Mom seemed to agree, but then she'd start the whole debate again.

Amelia and I watched a movie while my parents cooked dinner and talked about Shawn Weller. Every few seconds Amelia turned down the volume—not so much that they'd notice but enough so we could hear their conversation.

Mom said, "I've been coming to northern Wisconsin since I was a little girl. I wanted to sell the cabin because we had to. It was the responsible choice. Now that I know there could be another way, I'm just not sure."

Part of me wanted her to win this argument. Shawn Weller wasn't just selling the cabin. My best friend was part of the deal. Alex would no longer be my friend. But when I thought of digging up the money my ribs started squeezing the air right out of me. I heard Grumpa telling me to *let it rest* and it was like I was in the tunnel all over again.

"I have messages from Neil Clark to call him, and I can't." Dad slammed the cupboard. "You know why? Because I'd be embarrassed for him to know we're talking about Capone and the money right after the funeral."

"Todd, I have an idea. Just hear me out. We could hire a company to move the cabin. Then they could tear up the slab foundation and dig for the money. Then we rebuild the foundation and put the cabin back." Mom sounded so proud.

"That's a dangerous gamble. Basically we'd spend thousands and thousands of dollars for this long shot. What happens if we don't find a dime? Or say we do find money, but it's only a couple thousand dollars. We'd be in worse shape than we are now."

"I'm trying to think outside the box, Todd!"

"Here's another problem—the government! Capone went to jail for tax evasion. The government would probably confiscate the money for back taxes."

There was silence, and maybe tears, but mostly silence. Good. My ribs eased their grip on my chest a little. Amelia had just picked up the remote when Dad started talking again, softly this time.

"Honey? Do you really want to look for this money? I don't want you spending the rest of our lives wondering what might have happened. If it means that much to you, then let's just do it."

I bounced off the couch and shouted, "Why

can't you let it rest?" I went outside and slammed the door.

Alex was pretending to drive the ATV, which was perched on the driveway near the shed. Instead of a helmet, he had on Grumpa's fishing hat. He smiled and waved. I half-waved back and plopped down at our picnic table. Alex swung his leg off the ATV and walked slowly toward me.

"Christa, when do you think it'll be okay to play again?"

"You should ask that pastor. He seemed to know everything about dying."

"I didn't like him. I hated the whole thing. They put Grandpa in an ugly suit. How dumb was that?"

"I know!"

Alex flicked an ant off the bench and sat down. "Dad said my grandpa's heart was bad."

"It was not! He had a good heart."

"He didn't mean a bad heart like a bad person. He meant it wasn't working right."

"Oh." I was glad to know Neil didn't think Grumpa's heart was bad.

"Anyway, my dad is coming over to talk to your parents. He's been calling them since yesterday. Maybe they'll say it's okay for us to do something."

I sighed. "Maybe."

"Your legs look worse than mine." Alex stuck out his leg and we compared scratches.

"We look like road maps," I said.

"No. Road maps are orderly. This looks like someone tried to glue a cat to our legs."

The cabin door opened and Mom, Dad, and Amelia came outside. They said hello to Alex and asked him about his parents and talked about the weather. I figured they wanted to talk to me about the loot, but they didn't want to do it in front of Alex. An awkward moment, probably. But I didn't care. My chest was feeling tight, and I wanted to end it fast.

I interrupted all the weather talk. "Grumpa said the loot was cursed."

Dad looked surprised. He wiped his glasses on the bottom of his t-shirt. "Well, honey, a curse is an entertaining idea, but it's not real. Curses aren't real."

My head throbbed. Even though we were outside, there was not enough air to fill my lungs. I whispered, "Grumpa said we should let it rest! That's what he wanted." I blinked away tears—real tears. Eye sweats were for babies.

"I don't remember that," Alex said.

"It was in the library after you went upstairs. I don't want to talk about it again. Ever."

Mom covered her mouth with her hand. She blinked away tears, too, and pulled me into a hug. "We don't believe in curses, but we do believe in letting it rest. It's time to move on."

Neil spotted us from the Clarks' porch. He made his way over while Mom squeezed me. He said, "I'm sorry to just pop over like this, but it's important."

"Sorry I haven't returned your calls." Dad's face turned red. "It's been pretty crazy."

"I need to know if you signed the sale papers yet."

"The realtor is bringing them over," Dad said. "Why?"

"I talked to the investigators. Duncan's going to jail for a long time. Turns out he's been breaking into Capone's for years and stealing antiques. That's why the security systems never seemed to work. A cop knows how to get around them. Duncan even got Capone's personal handgun, which he sold to an unsuspecting collector for a fortune."

Dad shook his head. "That's terrible."

"A while ago, the insurance company for the property put up a reward leading to the arrest of the thief. The reward is twenty-five thousand dollars."

"Well, I'm glad they finally caught him. It's a shame it went on so long."

Neil leaned forward. "I don't think you heard me. There's a twenty-five thousand dollar reward."

Dad blinked a couple of times. "I don't get your point."

"The investigators say the reward money belongs to Amelia."

"Me?" Amelia's voice cracked.

Neil squeezed Alex's shoulders while he spoke. "You took Duncan down. You saved my son's life. I can't ever thank you enough, Amelia."

Dad's face went white. "Talk about a roller coaster of emotions. I think my head might explode."

"I know," Neil said. "It's a lot to think about. This week has been . . . well, it's been a week, hasn't it?"

"Can you excuse us for a moment?" Dad and Mom huddled by the cabin door and whispered. I'd never been both happy and sad at the same time, and those feelings did not get along. Those feelings made me tired.

Even if we kept our cabin, I'd never see Grumpa grumping on his front porch or fishing on the dock or napping in his recliner. No, it wouldn't be the same.

I watched Amelia as she straightened her *Eatsa Some Pizza* t-shirt and pulled her hair into a rubber band. She wasn't the same sister as two years ago, but she could still wrangle snakes. And now she could drive and stay up late and work at the best restaurant in the world.

I looked at Alex, who was picking at the scab on his knee. Next summer Alex My Friend might be Alex The Videogame Player or Alex The Best Friend Of Quincy. Or maybe he'd still be Buck Punch. But what if I wasn't Chase Truegood? I wasn't scared of anything except sharks and snakes, but I was afraid of everything being different. Everything was already different.

Finally, Mom and Dad came back to the picnic table. Mom said, "The reward money doesn't solve all our problems, but it goes a long way. We need to hear from Amelia. This involves her."

Amelia rumpled my hair. "Twenty-five thousand dollars would buy a lifetime supply of lip gloss."

I laughed and it felt good. Amelia's sense of humor was only ninety-nine percent gone. She could still be funny.

"We should use it for our family," Amelia said. "I didn't do anything special."

"You saved my life!" I punched her arm.

"Don't make me regret it."

"It's settled then," Mom said. "We're taking down the for-sale sign. We're staying."

"I'm glad to hear it," Neil said.

I hugged her hard. In my mind I hugged Grumpa next. Then I hugged Dad and Amelia and even Neil. I gave Alex a little punch in the arm.

Alex looked at his dad. "Is it okay if we go do something?"

"Sure. Go do something."

As Alex and I walked toward the shed, Mom called out, "Do not throw mud at Shawn Weller's sign!"

I put my hands on my hips and yelled back. "Jeez, Mom! We know! Of course we're not going to throw mud at the sign."

Alex adjusted Grumpa's fishing hat. "So what do you want to do?"

"Bummer," I said. "I really wanted to throw mud balls at that sign."

He sighed. "Me, too."